Missing In Bahia

Missing In Bahia

Will Grey

Writer's Showcase presented by *Writer's Digest*
San Jose New York Lincoln Shanghai

Missing In Bahia

Published by Writer's Showcase presented by *Writer's Digest*
an imprint of iUniverse.com, Inc.

For information address:
iUniverse.com, Inc.
620 North 48th Street
Suite 201
Lincoln, NE 68504-3467
www.iuniverse.com

ISBN: 0-595-00178-5

Printed in the United States of America

Dedication

Dedicated to the Black, Brown, and Beige women of the world, from Bahia to Boston, from Havana to Harare. For years you have been the inspiration of life and song, from Ellington to Motown, Marley to Mendez. Despite a lack of positive images in Western Media, your beauty, intelligence and strength have not gone unnoticed, and yes, you too deserve to be rescued by a prince.

Acknowledgements

This accomplishment is a result of many years of encouragement from family and friends. My sincere thanks to Mom, Dad, Royce, Joel, Tamara, Yvonne and all my fellow shipmates and soldiers in arms. I would like to give special thanks to Karen Taylor and Richard N. Côté for their outstanding editorial assistance.

Chapter 1

"Gurrrl, I can't even describe this guy, he was so fine. But if you had seen the butt on this man…umph! That was the first thing I saw, then he turned around and I almost fainted. Seriously. He was that fine."

Lauri lit a cigarette and blew the smoke into the air. Beverly's nose wrinkled in disgust as she moved further back on the sofa, fanning the air around her.

"Don't even start. You are at my house and the window's open. I don't smoke in your place, or in the car and I sit in the non-smoking section in restaurants with you. Now gimme a break, okay? Shoot. Now I lost my train of thought. Oh, right. David. So anyway, to make a long story short…"

"When have you ever made a long story short, Lauri? I don't even know why you say that. Look, I can't take the smoke for too long, so hurry up with the tawdry details so I can get outta here before you kill me."

Lauri rolled her eyes and stubbed out her cigarette. "Jeesh, can't even enjoy a cigarette in my own damn house," she muttered. "Anyway, so, I was trying to tell you we have a date."

Beverly leaned forward, punching Lauri on the arm. "You're kidding. Didn't you say he was with someone?"

Lauri had gotten up from the sofa and was heading for the bedroom. She turned to Beverly. "So? The point is, it can't have been too serious, because he sure made his way to my side to get my number. I am so glad I wore that little black dress. I swear, he talked to these babies the whole time." Lauri turned to the mirror and studied her reflection, pushing her breasts out further and smiling.

Beverly shook her head as Lauri disappeared into the bedroom.

"And," she shouted from the other room, "he'll be doing more than talking when he sees me in this." She emerged from the room a second later, holding a red dress on a hanger.

Beverly's eyes widened as she took the dress from Lauri. It was crushed velvet, micro-mini, with little spaghetti straps crisscrossing down the otherwise bare back.

"You have got to be kidding. Why don't you just meet him at the door buck-naked with a can of whipped cream? It'll be the same message."

"Humph." Lauri snatched the dress away from Beverly. "Cuz it's about subtlety."

"Right. That dress definitely says 'I want sex'—but subtly."

"You are such a prude. You know, it's a wonder you can keep a man like Mark. Shoot. If he was my man—"

"Well, he's not. So get off of it. I'm about to fire you as my maid of honor and let Mark hire you for the bachelor party."

"Why can't I do both? I've always wanted to be the surprise in the cake. And, I could tell you what you're getting into before you say 'I do.' You know, try the milk before you get the cow."

"In your dreams, sistah love. And only in your dreams. Now what kind of shoes are you wearing with that 'Tina Turner dress?"

Lauri raised her brow and grinned, "Girl, I have red, three inch killer spikes…

umph! He is going to drop to his knees…"

Beverly screamed. "Don't you dare—"

"…and beg me to marry him!" Lauri laughed uproariously. "Gotcha!"

Beverly chuckled. "You are unbalanced. I can't believe you are my best friend."

"Yes you can. And you know you're lucky to have me." Lauri looked furtively at her watch. "Uh…I'm hungry. Got anymore of that dinner you made last night?"

"Yeah, but no more chicken. Why don't we just go out to lunch, my treat?"

Lauri stood and lit another cigarette. With her back to Beverly, she said, "Nah, don't have time to go out for lunch. I'm…uh…expecting a phone call in about half an hour. Let's just go over to your place and make sandwiches."

"Girl, I'm going to start charging you for food. Let's order out. How about pizza?"

Lauri turned to Beverly, her mouth set in a frustrated frown. "But I'm hungry now. I don't want to wait for a delivery. Can't we just go and raid your fridge?"

Beverly sighed. "Fine. But you know, if you spent a little less money on those trashy dresses and a little more on groceries, you wouldn't get so damned cranky." She got up from the sofa and headed for the door.

Lauri stubbed her cigarette out and ran after Beverly. "Hey, wait for me."

Beverly turned to her. "Calm down. It's not like you're gonna get lost walking 10 feet down the hall to my place. Jeez."

"Well, I just want to make sure you don't get to the fridge before I do," Lauri shouted as they walked down the hall.

Beverly turned the handle on her apartment door and turned to Lauri. "Why are you shouting? D'you think I'm de—"

"SURPRISE!!" A chorus of women's voices rang out.

Lauri, a wide smile splitting over her face, pushed Beverly inside.

The living room had been transformed. Streamers and balloons in cream and coral, her wedding colors, hung from the ceiling. Her dining room table was covered with a coral tablecloth and was laden with platters of food. A second table had been set up beside it, this one covered with a cream-colored tablecloth and piled high with gifts.

Over the table was a hand-painted banner with a photograph of her face pasted over a woman's body. She was wearing a yoke and pulling a cart that held a man (with Mark's face pasted on the body) and six children. Underneath the picture, "Congrats—You're Getting Hitched!" was stenciled.

Beverly laughed at the picture as she scanned the faces of her friends. "Frances, I know you made that. Very funny."

Frances' plump, freckled face beamed with pride. "It took me over a week to get that done. It was Lauri's idea, though."

Beverly punched Lauri, then hugged her. "Figures."

"Congrats, Sis." Lauri hugged her back and then pushed her away. "Okay, enough of this. Where's the champagne?"

Glasses were quickly passed around. Lauri raised hers in the air and said, "Let the games begin! As Maid of Honor, I get the first toast!"

Chapter 2

Beverly sat in her office at Canterbury Enterprises, going over the final details for the morning meeting with her boss, Mr. Garrison, Stan Towers and the rest of the corporate team. It was a beautiful day, the sun was streaming through the vertical blinds, filling the room with light.

She was feeling great. The bridal shower had been a blast, and had gone on until almost 10:00 P.M., when she'd pushed the last guest out, so she and Lauri could clean up the mess. Beverly smiled as her mind wandered to the little black negligee Lauri had bought for her. Mark would die when he saw it. The phone rang.

"Beverly Madsen. Oh, Jean, hello. What can do for you?" She half-listened to the travel agent as she spotted an error on the report and corrected it.

"I haven't been able to reach Mr. Davis all week, and the airline reservations have to be ticketed today or we lose the rate."

Beverly put down her pen. "Pardon me?"

"The airline tickets. Well, the hotel needs to be confirmed too. I must say, Ms. Madsen, you've got a wonderful honeymoon planned. But as I said, the reservations have to be confirmed by credit card, today. I've left several messages for Mr. Davis, but he hasn't returned my calls. I'd hate to see you lose these rates."

"But Mark told me weeks ago that this was taken care of."

Jean's voice droned through the receiver. "Yes, well, he asked me to put together the package, which I did. I faxed the details over to him, but he never called back to confirm. I can't ticket without his authorization. Have you made other plans?"

There was a knock on Beverly's door. "Just a minute," she called out. "No. No, we haven't. At least, not that I know of."

The door opened and Stan Towers appeared, tapping his watch impatiently. "Let's go," he mouthed at Beverly.

Beverly waved him away. "Give me a sec, Stan. I'm coming. What time did you say, Jean?"

"Now," Stan said. "Garrison is already in there."

"Okay, okay." Beverly brushed her bangs from her forehead. "Look, Jean, I'll have to get back to you on this. Can I call you this afternoon?"

"Sure," Jean said, "but I have to ticket by close of business today or we lose those rates."

"I understand. Can I have your number?" Beverly jotted it down on the corner of her report. "Got it. I'll talk to you this afternoon. Thanks."

"Come on. You know how Garrison gets when he's kept waiting. And I have a great plan to pass by the old man. You are going to witness genius in action."

Beverly was still sitting at the desk, staring at the phone.

"Earth to Beverly, earth to Beverly, are you reading me? What was that call about?"

"Nothing." Beverly shook her head as she stood and gathered her papers. "Let's go."

• • •

"We can sell the property to Dashton in the first quarter, which will put us ahead of Liebermyer & Ross by a substantial margin."

Mr. Garrison smiled as he listened to his protégé, Stan Towers, complete his presentation. "Unload it now, write off the loss, and buy it back before close of the second quarter. Brilliant Stan. Just brilliant."

Beverly scanned the papers in front of her and then studied the numbers on the board before she spoke.

"And how do we explain the loss in the quarterly stockholders' report?"

Stan frowned at Beverly, then glanced quickly at Mr. Garrison as he considered a response.

"No one reads those reports anyway." Mr. Garrison waved his hand in dismissal.

"We'll just have Silverman & Klein do their usual number tricks for us. If there is no further business?" He glanced pointedly over the tops of his glasses at Beverly, and without waiting for an answer, pushed away from the table and strode from the conference room.

When the door closed behind him, Stan chuckled.

Beverly's brow knitted together in frustrated irritation. "Sure, go ahead and laugh. If I had presented that plan, Garrison would have thrown me out on my ear. 'No one reads those reports.' Right. We'll be up to our asses in lawsuits before the year is up and you know it. He knows it too, but you are his Golden Boy and as far as he's concerned, you can do no wrong." Beverly rested her face in her hands.

Stan laughed out loud as he pulled out the chair beside Beverly and sat.

"Listen. You're absolutely right, and Garrison is an idiot. But if things work out as I am anticipating, I'll get a big fat bonus on this deal and be off this sinking ship before the first papers are served."

"What are you talking about? What sinking ship?" Beverly sat up at full attention.

"Please. You have to know that Garrison is holding Canterbury together with spit and string. We've been operating at a loss for years. I'm telling you, this ship is sinking—and I mean fast. I, for one, have no intention of going down with her. If you're smart, you'll start making plans too."

Beverly twisted a curl around her finger as she considered this new information. "I had no idea. But what about Tierrasante? Their project promises to bring in millions to the firm."

Stan laughed again. "Look, if things work out the way I think they will, I'll be taking Tierrasante with me. Maybe," Stan paused, as if to consider, "if you are extra nice to me, I'll cut you in on the action. There is a lot of money to be made here."

Now Beverly smiled coyly. "And just how "nice" do I have to be?"

Stan stood. "Very nice. But for now, let's just keep this under our hats. Oh, and tell that boyfriend of yours, Mohammed, that you'll be working long hours with yours truly over the next few months."

"Mark." Beverly said distractedly.

"What?" Stan said.

"His name is not 'Mohammed.' It's Mark."

"Oh. Well, whatever. You know who I mean. You'd better start softening Mark up. We are going to be moving fast on this."

Beverly barely heard Stan's last words. The mention of Mark had released the worry she'd been holding in all morning. She felt her eyes sting with tears. She got up and gathered her papers together. Her back was turned away from Stan so he wouldn't see her upset and start asking questions she had no answers for.

"Uh, I've got a few calls to make. I'll catch up with you later on the Tierrasante project." With that, Beverly left the conference room, rushed back to her office and closed the door. It was not until she'd settled in her seat behind the desk, that tears began to fall.

Chapter 3

Beverly hadn't heard from Mark in over a month. He had come by that last night for dinner, and over a meal of linguine with clam sauce, citrus tossed spinach salad and homemade Italian garlic bread, he told her his squadron was being sent out on a mission.

"I can't tell you more than that. It's top secret. Hell, we don't even get all the details until we're in flight. I'll be incommunicado until it's finished." He poured them both another glass of wine.

Beverly looked across the candlelit table at her fiancé. "How long do you think you'll be gone this time? There's so much we need to finalize before the wedding."

Mark smiled his most charming smile as he lifted his glass and took a sip.

"Don't worry, baby. Everything is taken care of. I've made all the arrangements for the honeymoon, which you are going to love, my tuxedo awaits final alterations, which I'll do when I get back. We don't move into the new place for another six weeks, and my apartment is almost packed up—not that I had that much to pack. All that I have left to do is have my wild bachelor party and show up on the appointed day with a hangover." He laughed.

Beverly laughed too. "You'd better show up at that altar sober. Because sober or not, those vows are binding and you are not getting out of it by pleading temporary insanity."

Her smile faded. She added softly, "I'm going to miss you, Mark. You'd better not get hurt or find someone more exciting and beautiful to fall in love with either."

Mark stood and pulled Beverly to her feet, kissing her gently. "There is no one else for me, Bev. Don't you know that? I want to go to bed with you every night. Wake up to you every morning. You are the woman that will welcome me home, have my children, be my friend and lover. Okay?"

Tears welled in Beverly's eyes. She brushed them away as she studied Mark's face. Trying to smile, she said, "Yeah? Well, you'd better not forget that, Mark Davis."

Mark pulled Beverly closer, kissing her more passionately. "I won't. I can't."

Beverly felt her body responding to Mark's urgency, and she whispered, "Do you still want dessert?"

Mark smiled as he took Beverly's hand and looked to the bedroom. "That was exactly what I was thinking. A little dessert about now is just what I need."

Beverly blew out the candles on the table and allowed Mark to lead her to the bedroom, turning out the lights as they went. Beverly smiled too. "Then just wait and see what I've cooked up for you."

• • •

They'd made love all night, and then fell asleep in each other's arms, the passion-dampened sheets tangled around their legs.

In the morning, when Beverly's alarm went off, Mark was gone. He'd left her a note telling her he had to be at headquarters at 06:00 hours and hadn't wanted to wake her. He closed the note by telling her he loved her and would see her soon.

But two weeks had passed. And then three, and there was no word from Mark. Beverly called Mark's mother, but she told Beverly that she didn't have any information. As Beverly hung up the phone, she sensed that Mrs. Davis wasn't telling her the truth. After that call, Mrs. Davis hadn't returned any of Beverly's messages.

Over a month had passed and still no word from Mark. And now the travel agent was calling to confirm their honeymoon plans, and Beverly wasn't certain there would be a wedding.

Beverly felt the stirrings of fear in her stomach. Despite Mark's reassurances, she was wondering if perhaps he had found someone else. Maybe he was leaving her at the altar. Surely she would have been notified if something had happened to Mark, so it couldn't be that. And she knew that Mark had always had an eye for women, how could she have believed he had changed?

She remembered him in college, always with a different woman on his arm. He was charming, handsome and sexy. She felt an instant attraction to him when Dexter introduced them, back in sophomore year.

Dexter. Her childhood friend and sweetheart. Everyone thought they'd eventually get married. She had believed it too, until she met Mark. In Dexter, Beverly knew she'd have security, safety and love. They would have had a good life, the life she was raised to live. Family, friends, trips to Disney World, summer barbecues and a vegetable garden out back. And then he'd introduced her to his best friend. Mark Davis.

Beverly couldn't describe the feeling she got, being with Mark. Part of the attraction, she knew, was his sense of adventure. He represented a life of excitement, a passion different from what she'd ever known, would ever know, with Dexter.

She and Dexter broke up later that year, but remained friends. Still, she stayed away from Mark. He was, after all, Dexter's best friend, and Beverly loved Dexter too much to hurt him that way.

It wasn't until after college, when Dexter and Mark had joined the Navy, that things changed. They'd all get together whenever time permitted, for dinner, laughs, sometimes with dates, sometimes just the three of them. And then, one weekend, Mark came home alone.

They'd met for dinner, as usual, but without Dexter there, there was no buffer, no distraction from the current of attraction that pulsed between them. They barely finished dinner, before they silently agreed to go back to her place and explore their feelings. They'd spent the weekend in her bed.

Dexter had been surprised to hear they were together, but if he was hurt, he concealed it well. It had been, after all, several years since he and Beverly had been an item. He wished them well.

But after that, he never seemed to be on leave the same time as Mark. The two of them, she and Dexter, still got together from time to time, but it was never the three of them again. Beverly accepted a job with Canterbury Enterprises in Philadelphia. She moved there at about the same time Dexter joined the Secret Service. He claimed his work kept him from keeping in closer touch. By the time Mark asked Beverly to marry him, she only heard from Dexter on birthdays and Christmas, when he sent her a card and gift.

Beverly kept up with his life and successes through his mother, who still lived down the street from her folks. Beverly flipped through her phone book and found his home number. If anyone could find Mark, it was Dexter. She picked up the phone and then hesitated.

What would she say to him after so long? She knew that part of his estrangement was because of Mark, but surely he would help her. Her eyes fell on the hastily jotted number of the travel agent. She just had to know what had happened to Mark. Taking a deep breath, she dialed Dexter's number.

Chapter 4

Mark walked into the back room of the hangar. The room was small, hot and cluttered. He dropped is logbook on the desk and sat heavily. *Too many late nights and early morning runs,* he thought to himself. *I'm getting too old for this.*

He picked up a dusty picture frame that was propped up against a stack of magazines on the corner of his desk. He looked at the man he used to be. Dressed in a khaki-colored, silk tee shirt that accentuated his muscled chest, the man was grinning widely and showing off his bulging biceps. His other arm was draped over his fiancée, Beverly Madsen.

They looked good together. His dark chocolate, smooth skin and neatly cropped faded haircut made a striking contrast to Beverly's bronzed goddess good looks. She was wearing a coral-colored slip dress, which clung to her firm breasts and full hips as if designed with only her in mind. Sandy colored, natural curls cascaded over her shoulders and midway down her back. Her face was in profile, and Mark smiled sadly, recalling that Beverly had just stolen a kiss from his cheek when the picture was snapped.

That had been almost two years ago, on a romantic weekend getaway they'd taken just after Mark had asked Beverly to be his wife.

So much had happened since then. The secret mission he'd flown for his country had gone terribly wrong and he had been made the scapegoat. The reality of his disposability to his government shook him to his core as he stood at attention at his shotgun court martial.

Beverly had stood by him through the ordeal, but not even her love could wash away the bitterness. Finally, Mark decided to take off. He determined to leave the United States for good and start his life over.

He remembered the last night he'd spent with Beverly. He had not been able to tell her he was leaving as he'd planned. He looked into her beautiful face, so loving and trusting, and couldn't bring himself to break her heart. They'd made love that night, and Mark had tried to convey through his body, all that he loved and knew he'd be losing. He got up in the pre-dawn hours and watched her sleeping. Then he quietly got dressed, left her a note and after kissing her good bye, slipped out of the apartment. Part of him felt like a coward, the other part, the part he clung to, knew that it was for the best.

So here he was, flying pre-dawn deliveries in the small Brazilian town of Ilhéus, Bahia. Instead of arguing with Beverly about whose belongings would go where in their new house with pool and deck, Mark's "home" was a run-down, two room cottage, one half mile from this small tourist airport. The house had no air conditioning, no TV and little furniture, other than a thin twin mattress and a tattered sofa covered with an old army blanket.

And instead of anticipating Beverly's smooth, Estee-perfumed body curling around him each night, he was going home to Caterina. A beautiful and sexy Cuban exile, who didn't get herbal body wraps and weekly manicures. Her beauty was smoky, seductive and natural. She was passionate and honest. But most of all, she had no ties to the life he'd left behind. He studied Beverly's face again. That was another life. Another life, dead and gone. He stuffed the picture into the battered drawer of his desk and closed it—and Beverly—from his mind.

He had made his choice. It was better for everyone, certainly for him, that he start his life over here, in this out-of-the-way, dusty dot on the map, far from the typical American tourist highways. His needs were simple, and they were adequately met in this sleepy seaside town that reminded him of home.

Getting up with a groan, he stretched. The muscles in his wide, strong shoulders and arms flexed long and hard. The ceiling was low in the little office, and his six-foot, three-inch frame filled the space, his hands, stretched above his head, lay flat against the ceiling. Taking a bandana from his back pocket, Mark wiped the sweat from his brow and then tossed it on the desk.

Sabo Bolatti, owner of the airstrip, stomped into the office, a half-eaten caju fruit in his hand. "What the hell did you think you were doing out there this morning?"

Mark leaned against the desk, crossing his arms. "What are you talking about?"

"You know exactly what I'm talking about. I just got a call from the Policia Militar. Did you buzz that war bird over Cristo beach?"

Mark smiled slightly and studied Sabo under hooded eyes. After a minute, he shrugged nonchalantly, but said nothing.

"You fool," Sabo continued furiously, "they will take my license because of your stupidity."

Mark picked up a magazine from the desk and flipped through it nonchalantly, not looking up as he answered, "Relax Sabo. If I weren't working out of this sad excuse for an airport, Brasilia would have closed you down months ago. So give it a rest."

"Damned gringo," Sabo muttered. "Mr. Goessel called again. He wants to know when you will be finished testing the Puma."

Mark tossed the magazine aside and stood. "When he pays me what he owes."

Sabo put the caju fruit remains on the desk and pulled out a cigar, lighting it nervously. "I can't tell him that. You just get it done."

Mark brushed by him. "Tell him it's got a bad gyro. Which it will, and which won't be repaired until I get what I'm owed."

Sabo sputtered as he watched Mark's departing figure. "Where are you going? We are not finished here."

Mark tossed over his shoulder, "Yes, we are. I'm beat. I'm going home to get some sleep. As for the good German, tell him whatever you want to Sabo. You know where I stand. I'll be back at four."

Chapter 5

Mark shoved his hands into his pockets and strolled past Sabo, and continued walking down the road, away from the strip. He was exhausted, but too restless to go back to his room. He looked up at the sky, a deep blue, dotted with streaks of pale white clouds. It would be a scorching day.

He made his way down the dirt road, the usually verdant, flowered bushes that decorated the road, already wilting in the early morning heat, their scent heavy and slightly burnt.

Cutting through the brush, he found the path he had trodden down on this, his short cut down to the ocean. For a little while, the only sounds he heard were the cicadas and the colorful parrots. In this silence, this private piece of paradise, he felt himself start to relax a bit. He widened his stride, now an easy lope. He was free here. Free from false expectations and dashed ideals. Free from playing games he once thought he could win.

The sound of the ocean, and the laughter of children, brought him back from his gloomy thoughts. He pushed them back down, as he broke through the bushes and stepped onto the dune that overlooked Ilhéus' small strip of sandy beach lining the immense ocean.

There were several native bathers lounging in the sand, shouting at children playing in the surf, talking and laughing in their silky Portuguese. There were no American tourists on this beach, they preferring the busier, noisier beaches of Rio. That was fine with Mark. He took in the beautiful browns of the children, chasing a ball and splashing each other, loud yelps of laughter carrying over the ocean breeze to Mark.

This was one of the reasons Mark had chosen this place. The native Bahians were warm and generous. They had not succumbed to the hectic, materialistic lifestyle Mark saw exported by America and Europe and rapidly overtaking their São Paulo and Rio brethren. The Northeast was still an innocent, refreshing Brazil. From the darkest chocolate to pale and freckled; hair in tight kinks to tousled curls, the Bahians bore a similar genetic heritage to black Americans, and this, gave him comfort so that this self imposed exile was not so lonely.

And of course, there was Caterina. Mark sat in the sand and took off his canvas shoes, placing them beside him. Caterina. She was certainly not something Mark had planned. He shook his head ruefully. He had met Caterina on his second day in Ilhéus. He could remember just how they'd met.

He had been so filled with anger with the country that had turned it's back on him, as surely as he was now turning his back on it and remorse about how he had left Beverly. It was all he could do to check into the anonymous hostel, dump his duffel bag and sleep.

That second day, while talking haltingly with the old man who ran the place, a beautiful young woman came out of the office, slipping her arm around the old man with a warm smile, and then turning a haughty, cool gaze on him. Mark had put on his most charming face, nodding acknowledgment to her and raising one brow rakishly, which never failed to win the ladies. She sniffed at him, turning back to the old man. She whispered something in his ear and then turned and walked stiff-backed back into the office. She shut the door firmly behind her, but not before giving Mark a baleful look, followed by a slightly amused smile.

He saw her again, later that afternoon, as he toured the sleepy little town. He had wandered aimlessly down the narrow streets, enjoying the hardness of the dirt and cobble road under his shoes, taking in the white-washed, ancient stone houses. Shutters were painted in bright yellows and reds, lace curtains blowing out of open windows, further decorated with window boxes filled with brightly colored flowers.

He ended at a quiet square, enclosed by sandy-colored stone wall, which opened to a pathway flanked by the low walls, on the other side. Intrigued, Mark followed it, enjoying the dappled sunlight that filtered through the lush, overhanging trees, and came upon a sandstone archway. Passing under it, he came upon the town's open-air marketplace. It was teeming with people in straw hats and bandana draped heads, stalls of fruit and fish and meats; colorful blankets and tourist trinkets.

Mark smiled as he watched the bustling activity. Brazil had something Mark loved. The people were full of life, as lively as the coconut palmed beaches of Ilhéus suggested to tourists. More importantly, the colors of Bahians reminded Mark of home. From bittersweet chocolate to bronze; cinnamon to beige. The women had the curves found only on women with African descent in their blood. The sweet pulsating sounds of Samba and Bossa Nova filled the air. Bahians considered themselves the heart and soul of Brazil, and Mark loved it. No one questioned whether he was black or white or purple in Brazil. As far as they were concerned, he looked Brazilian, though he sounded and dressed American.

Beyond the chaos of the masses of noisy people, the smoke from open pits of steaming meat and seafood, manned by sweaty, shouting vendors, was the ocean. It was clear, still and brilliantly blue. Mark stared at it, entranced.

"It seems impossible—the ocean so quiet and peaceful, just steps away from all of this."

Mark turned. Caterina stood just behind him, looking out at the ocean. She was carrying a basket over her arm, her curly, black hair was pulled back into a ponytail with a bright scarf. She was wearing a white, cotton tank top. Its scooped neck was decorated with colorful threads embroidered in a vine of flowers. Mark couldn't help but notice that, although the shirt was worn loose fitting, the fabric was thin enough to just make out the outline of her small, up-turned breasts. The top was tucked into a long, peach-colored, gauzy skirt, a beaded hemp belt cinching her small waist. She was wearing sandals. No polish, no jewelry, no makeup. She was beautiful.

"I had no idea there were so many people in this little town." Mark rumbled in his deepest, Barry White voice, as he flashed his signature smile.

Caterina turned to him. "Senhor, you have not been here long enough to know anything about this place or its people." She turned her face back towards the ocean and was silent. A breeze picked up the curled strands of dark hair framing her face and brushed them across her forehead and neck.

Mark was taken aback. It was the first time any woman had not immediately responded to his charms, even a bit. He quickly thought about how he might proceed, smiling to himself at the challenge that was this woman, when Caterina spoke again.

"If you will promise not to try and charm me with your American…how do you say…*come ons*, and," she added with a smile, "if you will carry my basket, you can walk with me down to the beach. There is a cove down there where, they say, one can hear the echoes of the song thirty Africans sang as they walked into the sea, giving their lives to *Yemaya*, rather than endure the chains of slavery." She handed Mark the basket and started down the path.

Mark grinned as he took the basket and followed Caterina, admiring the musical sway of her hips as she moved down the hill.

• • •

Mark smiled at the memory. Caterina had stayed with him that night and most nights after that. He was never quite sure of what it was that had finally won her over. She was quick and witty in her conversation, energetic and uninhibited in bed. From time to time, Mark felt a twinge of guilt, after all, he had left a beautiful bride behind in the States. Then he'd turn and see Caterina sleeping beside him.

She didn't seem to want anything from Mark, except a little companionship. She never asked about his relationships back home or how long he'd be around Ilhéus. She always left just before dawn, so she could get changed and have breakfast with the old man—her father, he learned. She didn't talk much about herself and she never left any of her things behind, like most women did when they wanted to lay claim to a man.

She was a safe haven of comfort at a time when Mark really needed it. *Anyway*, he reasoned, *he wasn't actually engaged anymore.* Eventually, Beverly would get over him (though never forget him), marry someone else and her life would go on, so it wasn't as if he were being unfaithful.

The children's dog came bounding up to Mark, shaking cold ocean water all over him, in doggy exuberance and pulling him out of his daydream. Mark waved at the children and joined their laughter. Then he picked up a stick, throwing it far down the beach, and the dog raced away after it. It was getting late. He really needed to get some sleep before he returned to the airstrip at four.

Mark picked up his shoes and stood. *Yeah, life goes on*, he thought with a heavy sigh. With a last look at the ocean, Mark turned and headed home.

Chapter 6

The phone rang, bringing Beverly out of her reverie. For a moment, she hesitated. What if it were Dexter, calling her back? She took a deep breath and picked up the phone on the second ring. "Beverly Madsen, may I help you?"

It was Lauri. "Hey girl, what's going on?"

Beverly turned her chair towards the window and stared out into the bright day. "Alright, I guess. I, uh…I got a call from the travel agent about the honeymoon plans."

"Cool. So did Mark give in and tell you where you're going?"

Beverly's eyes watered. "She, uh…she called because Mark hadn't confirmed the tickets. She wanted to know if we had made other plans."

"Say what?" Lauri's voice boomed through the receiver. "I don't believe this. That trifling brother. All he had to do was book the honeymoon and he didn't do it? I hope you called him and cussed him out."

"Lauri…I…uh…," Beverly started crying.

"What's wrong? Hey, Bev, what's going on?" Lauri's voice had risen in alarm.

"Lauri, I haven't talked to Mark in over a month. Remember I told you he was going on some secret mission? Well, either he hasn't come back yet, or he *has* come back and just hasn't…"

"Hey, hey. Okay. Listen, you wanna meet? I can come down and, and we'll have lunch or just talk." She paused, as she listened to Beverly's quiet gasps for air.

"I don't know why you're worrying. You know Mark is crazy about you. And you said he couldn't call until the job was done. It must be taking longer than he expected. Right? It happens. Bev?"

Beverly grabbed a tissue from her top desk drawer, and dabbed her eyes. "Yes, I know." She sniffed and took a deep breath, regaining control. In a voice more steady, she continued, "I don't know why I'm so worried. It's just that we are really coming down to the wire and I'm nervous. And his mother won't talk to me and I know she knows something." She took a deep breath before continuing. "I called Dexter."

There was silence on the line for a moment. Then Lauri said quietly, "You called Dexter?"

Beverly got defensive. "I figured he could find out what was going on. Lauri, I need to know what's going on. I've been going crazy for weeks."

"Why didn't you tell me any of this before? Why'd you think you had to go through this alone? For Pete's sake, Bev, I'm your best friend."

"I know. And I'm sorry. It's just that, well, I didn't know if I was being ridiculous about this whole thing. I started worrying about all of Mark's women, thinking maybe he was having second thoughts—I was trying to handle it. But then the travel agent called…and…I got scared. I didn't know what to do."

Lauri's voice was cautious. "And what did old Dexter have to say?"

Beverly sighed. "Nothing. I mean, I left him a message on his home machine. I thought this call might have been him."

"Well, you just be careful. D'you hear me? Cuz whether you want to admit it or not, Dexter still has the hots for you. This is just the kind of thing that could cause a situation. Listen. I'll come over and bring lunch. You know, be moral support when he calls."

"That won't be necessary, Lauri. But thanks. I'll tell you about it tonight—if I hear from him. But I don't know what to do about the tickets."

"Girl, you'd better get those tickets. You have a honeymoon coming up. And if the worst scenario happens, which I am not saying it will, you are gonna need a vacation anyway. Where are you going?"

"I don't know. I was so flustered when Jean called, I forgot to ask." There was a knock on her door. "Listen, hon, I have to run. There's someone at my door. We'll talk tonight, okay?"

Lauri answered reluctantly. "Well, alright. But you come by my apartment first thing when you get in—or I am coming over to you. Deal?"

"Deal. And Lauri? Thanks. I love you."

"Yeah, I know. I'll talk to you later."

As Beverly hung up the phone, the door to her office opened. It was Eric Thompson, a junior member of the corporate team.

"Got a minute?"

Beverly waved him in and motioned to the chair. "Have a seat. What can I do for you, Eric?"

"Stan the man does it again, huh? Faster than a speeding bullet, more powerful than a Wharton MBA."

Beverly looked sternly at Eric. "Look, I'm pretty busy, Eric. Do you mind getting to the point?"

Eric smoothed the crease in his trousers. "Stan pulled another fast one today, didn't he? He'd steal a piece of candy from a baby if he could get away with it. That son of a bitch sold more properties than any of us in the last two quarters combined. Think his pops is feeding him clients?"

"So what if he is? Stan is sharp and he's got connections, which he is not afraid to use. Your point?"

"Geez, Bev. Why are you all of a sudden the president of the Stan Towers' fan club? Is there something going on here that I should know about?"

"I'm just sick of the 'lets slam Stan" show around here. He's good at what he does, and he's not going to change for anyone who isn't signing his check. So I ask you again, what's your point?"

Eric started to answer, when the phone rang. Beverly picked it up. "Beverly Madsen." A slow smile spread across Beverly's face. In a voice warm and deep, she said, "Dexter. Hi. I'm so glad you returned my call." She looked across at Eric watching her. "Hold a minute, will you?"

Putting a hand over the receiver, Beverly said brusquely, "Eric, if there's nothing else, I'll talk with you later."

Eric's face turned red at the dismissal. "Of course. We'll talk later." He got up quickly and left the office. When the door closed behind him, Beverly returned to her call.

"You were saying?"

Dexter's voice sounded strong, confident. Beverly felt herself relaxing into it, her insides warming with its familiarity.

"I was asking how you've been?" His voice was wistful as he continued. "It's been a long time, Bev."

"I know. It has been. Too long, Dex. I've missed you." Her voice was low, almost a whisper.

There was a pause, and then Dexter continued, the softness in his voice gone as he asked, "and how is Mark? I haven't talked to him in a while either."

Beverly suddenly remembered why she'd called him. "Dexter, Mark is…I think…I…I haven't heard from Mark in several weeks. He went on a mission or something over a month ago. He told me he wouldn't be able to contact me until it was done, but I haven't heard from him since. I was…." her voice broke, "I was hoping you could find out what happened to him?"

There was silence on the line, and Beverly, suddenly nervous, rushed on. "I didn't know who else to ask. His mother won't talk to me and the wedding is less than a month away. I don't know if he's missing or….or if he's just decided to leave me. I…I didn't know who else to call."

Dexter took a deep breath and said, "Listen Bev, I'll make a few calls, see what I can find out. If he's on a Black Ops mission, I won't be able to get any information, but we'll see, okay?"

"Dexter, thank you. I knew I could count on you. Thank you."

"No promises, so don't go thanking me yet. I said I'll try." Dexter continued, "Listen, I have a meeting in Philly tomorrow morning. Why don't we have dinner tonight? I'll fill you in on what I find, and you can fill me in on you...and...the wedding. Deal?"

Beverly heard the hurt in Dexter's voice, and answered gently, "It's been a long time, Dex, I'd like that. Say, why don't we meet at Zanzibar Blue? Is seven-thirty alright for you?"

"Sounds good. And Bev? I'll find out what I can about Mark. It's good to hear your voice again. See you soon. Take care."

As Beverly hung up the phone, she pictured Dexter's face and her heart ached. She knew he still loved her—and she loved him too, just not the way he needed her to. She pondered on the mysteries of life and love, hoped he would get answers about Mark and wondered if his smile still lit up his eyes the way it had so many years before.

Chapter 7

Beverly absent-mindedly doodled pictures on her pad, while she contemplated where her life was. Only the night before, she had been the brunt of good-natured ribbing by her friends as they toasted her wedding. She'd opened boxes of lingerie and small appliances intended to make her transition to married life easier. Someone had even given her one of those Zen-like water fountains, with advice to meditate with it before she got into her first argument as a married woman.

Everyone had laughed when Lauri dismissed the fountain, saying "Forget that rock garden. A frying pan to the head has worked as an argument ender for hundreds of years. You won't really hurt Mark, his head is made of granite!"

Well, Beverly worried, *I sure hope Lauri is right about Mark's invincibility.* What if Mark had been horribly injured on that mission and was in some hospital somewhere? But surely someone would have notified her? Then again, maybe not. They weren't married yet. But what if he was fine, and had just decided not to come back to her? Maybe he met someone beautiful and daring out there—wherever he was—and had decided that Beverly wasn't the one after all?

Beverly threw the pen on the desk and rested her face in her hands for a moment, and then took a deep breath and pushed away from the desk, turning her chair to the window, studying the people rushing around taking care of business.

That's what she needed to do. Take care of business. Beverly stood. After all, she had called Dexter for help and he'd promised to look into the matter. Her switchboard had been informed to find her, no matter what she was doing, or where she was, if a call came in from Mark; and her home phone had been forwarded to her office so she wouldn't miss his call there either. That was all she could humanly do. In the meanwhile, she had enough work on her desk to keep her mind occupied.

Sitting down at her desk again, Beverly reached for her Rolodex, when the door opened and Stan slipped in. Usually, the six-foot tall, blond hair and blue eyed Stan, with his Italian designed suits and impeccably tooled and maintained hand-stitched loafers, looked like a model out of *GQ*. But standing there, his back against the door, his face split with a sneaky grin, looked more like a five-year-old who had just put a tack in his teacher's chair. Beverly couldn't help smiling. "What is it?" she laughed.

Stan's smile widened. "Old Garrison just left the office for a meeting. I want to show you something. Come on."

Beverly felt like a den mother. "Stan, I don't have time for games right now—"

Stan took another step towards her desk. "Well, you'd better make time for *this* game, because this is the Game of Life. Your life. Let's go." He turned and opened the door again.

Beverly, her brows raised in question, shrugged as she stood and followed him.

• • •

Stan closed the conference room doors behind them and ushered Beverly over to the table where a scaled model of a town was on display. He stood back silently as Beverly walked slowly around it.

"So this is it? Colonnade? It looks like its own city."

Stan smiled. "It is. Tierrasante has taken the dreams of the middle class and made them manifest in communities like this one, all over the country."

Beverly took in the tiny Victorian homes, the landscaped park areas, restaurants and stores. There was a school, and even a movie theatre. "This is amazing. I had no idea."

"It is amazing. And each village has a private police force, commissioned directly by the residents. Last year, the National Association of Police Chiefs and Law Enforcement Officials declared the Tierrasante communities the safest in the nation."

Stan pointed to the model of the school. "And, each village has its own private school system. These schools have produced outstanding results. Why, in Tierrasante's first community, Paradise Valley, which opened only four years ago, the students SAT/ACT scores ranged overall in the 97the percentile. Nationally, the Tierrasante school system students accounted for 2% of the freshman classes at Stamford, Princeton and Harvard this year."

Beverly moved away from the model and sat on the windowsill, looking out on the city. Stan joined her. "Because of the incredible success of the four villages they have constructed so far, Tierrasante plans on building communities all over the country. They are moving fast. They need smart people to move with them. They've got me, Bev. And I want you."

Beverly looked up at Stan, concern etched between her brows. "I would be lying if I said I wasn't intrigued. But, Stan, what about Canterbury? Mr. Garrison? This deal, if it really is as great as you are making it sound, would save this company and still make us a lot of money. Why cut him out after all he's done for you—for us?"

Stan stood, shoving his hands into his pockets. "Look. Garrison is through. That's all there is to it. The question is not how to save him, it's how to save yourself. Tierrasante is leaving this firm, and they are taking the project with them. That's a done deal. They are going to put these communities up. That is also a fact. The question you have to answer is, are you in—or out?"

Beverly bit her bottom lip as she considered Stan's words. Stan cut into her thoughts. "Look. I'm having lunch with Greg Young this afternoon. He is the head of Tierrasante's U.S. operations. Why don't you join us?" Stan sat beside Beverly and took her hand again.

"You're good, Beverly. And smart. Don't let sentimentality get in the way of a business decision that could make your future." He handed Beverly a bound report.

"Look this over. It outlines the entire project, what they've done to date and where they are heading. Then talk with Young before you decide. Okay?" Stan stood.

"Meet me in the lobby in about an hour. We'll go over to the restaurant together. At the very least, you'll get a great meal. What do you say?"

Beverly looked up at Stan and smiled. "Well, I am hungry."

Chapter 8

Young picked up his drink and took a long swallow. Glaring at the television set behind the bar, he pulling out his phone, dialed a number and waited, his eyes narrowed as the television reporter continued commenting on the upcoming elections. "What the devil's going on? I just saw the news...Yes, I'm sure you are...Where is Edward? Well find out!" He disconnected the line, as Stan and Beverly walked in. A pleasant smile replaced the scowl of a moment ago, as he stood and took Stan's hand.

"Stan, good to see you." He looked at Beverly appreciatively and then back to Stan.

"Mr. Young, it is a pleasure to introduce you to the woman I spoke to you about earlier. This is Beverly Madsen, one of our top corporate real estate pros. I've talked to her about Tierrasante's community project and she's very interested."

Young studied Beverly's face closely, then took her hand. "A pleasure, Ms. Madsen. And please, call me Greg. Stan has spoken very highly of you. I'm pleased that you are considering joining our team."

Beverly withdrew her hand with a slight smile. "Stan has told me quite a bit about the project, and I am interested in hearing more about its possibilities."

Young nodded his head. "I see. Well, why don't we talk about it over lunch? Our table is waiting." He put his hand on the small of Beverly's back and escorted her into the dining room.

Over lunch, Young and Stan talked about the ground breaking in Chicago and their meeting with Detroit investors. Beverly sat back and studied Mr. Gregory Young.

Noting his hand-tailored suit and monogrammed linen shirt, gold cufflinks and tie pin. She acknowledged that he was the picture of affluence, power and success. Not a tall man, perhaps five foot, seven inches, Greg Young looked to be in his late forties. His sharp features, translucent skin and ruddy cheeks suggested that he was Anglo.

Beverly surmised as she took in the broken blood vessels on his nose, that this was a man who had probably spent a good deal of his youth drinking a lot of cheap liquor. His hair was a nondescript, muddy auburn, sprinkled with gray, but freshly cut and carefully groomed. His hands were large, and though manicured, had the look of a rough-hewn look of a former laborer.

He probably built this empire up from nothing, she thought admiringly. She watched him as he rehashed a recent meeting to Stan. He spoke with the smug confidence of one who is used to being listened to. His gestures were a little arrogant, but Beverly decided that she found him charming. Here was a man who looked as if he started at the very bottom and was now leading a multi-million dollar real estate conglomerate that was changing the very way people's lives would be lived.

Beverly felt drawn in by both his sincere enthusiasm for the project, and his descriptions of the wealth and position that could be had as a member of the Tierrasante team.

The waiter poured more coffee and removed the emptied lunch plates. Placing the bill face down on the table, he said, "If there's nothing else, I'll take your check when you're ready. No rush, just let me know."

Stan nodded with a slight smile and then turned back to Young. "Tierrasante is a very dynamic company, Greg."

Young folded his hands together and rested them on the table, leaning forward earnestly. "Yes, sometimes even I am amazed at how the concept has grown so rapidly. You have gotten in at a great time, Stan."

He turned to Beverly, "And what do you think, Ms. Madsen? We have plenty of room for pros of your caliber. I understand you are one of the brightest at Canterbury."

Beverly blushed modestly. "Please, call me Beverly. "I've scanned the specs Stan gave me on the company and the project outlines, and certainly, if Stan's—" she looked at Stan with a smile, "if Stan's stories are to be believed, I'd have to admit that I'd be a fool not to want to be a part of this project. I like what it offers to its residents and I like what it does for the surrounding communities."

Beverly paused, "But I need to think about this a little more. There is the issue of Canterbury Enterprises. Canterbury has done well by me. And if I am good at what I do, it's because of Mr. Garrison's mentoring and the opportunities he has afforded me.

"That's why I'm not comfortable with just walking out on him and Canterbury. Mr. Young—Greg," Beverly smiled, "I feel obligated to ask you to reconsider your decision to take Tierrasante and this project away from Canterbury. I think we can meet your needs, particularly with Stan and me heading up the team there.

"We have something valuable to offer that Tierrasante has not yet fully developed—and that is a long-standing and trusted reputation here in the Philadelphia area and, to a lesser degree, throughout the northeastern corridor.

"Tierrasante hasn't established itself here in the Valley and it takes some time to build trust, particularly among the old money here which, I understand, is the target market for these projects."

Stan sighed impatiently. "I've told you that Canterbury is just too small time to accommodate the national vision of Tierrasante, Bev, and as for the "old monied," we take our reputations with us to Tierrasante. That, the contacts I have, thanks to old Pops, and the phenomenal package that Tierrasante offers its citizens, will be more than enough to bring in the old guard."

Mr. Young put his hand up, "Stan, I respect Beverly's loyalty to her company. It is rare to find in these days of buy-outs and mergers."

Young turned back to Beverly again. "Canterbury is a fine company, Ms. Madsen. And I have a lot of respect for Emmanuel Garrison. But Stan is right. It just doesn't have the scope or reach we need to make the Tierrasante communities what we envision. It is unfortunate, but that is the way it is. We are going on without Canterbury, and we'd like you to be with us on this adventure. So please, do consider our offer seriously. You'd be a real asset to our organization."

Beverly answered firmly, "Thank you, Greg I do appreciate the offer. But this is a big decision. I'd like to think about it for a day or two, if I may."

Young pulled out his wallet, and handed a credit card to the waiter. "Certainly Beverly. I understand and I do appreciate your position. Might I suggest you join us for the investors meeting this evening? You'll get a better idea of the people involved right here in your community."

"I'm afraid I've already made other plans this evening that can't be cancelled. I would, however, like very much to attend one of those meetings."

Stan jumped in. "We're meeting with investors on the Detroit project on Thursday. Why don't you fly out with me for the day, take a look at the site and sit in on the meeting?"

"Well…I…"

"Well you, nothing. Tierrasante is Canterbury's biggest client, *for now,*" Stan smirked. "Garrison will dance the jig at the additional billing you'll generate by coming along."

Beverly nodded. "Well, when you put it that way." She turned to Young and offered her hand, which he took and shook briefly. "Then it's settled. I'll see you in Detroit. Now, if you'll excuse me, I have a few loose ends to tie up at the office before my meeting."

Young and Stan stood as she got up from the table. Young took her hand again. "I am looking forward to working with you, Ms. Madsen."

Beverly nodded her head at Young, then Stan. "If you'll excuse me." She turned and walked out.

When she was gone, Young turned to Stan, his pleasant demeanor replaced by irritation. "You do not make decisions on behalf of Tierrasante, Mr. Towers. If you have any other bright ideas about bringing people into this, you come to me first, understand?"

Stan's face turned red. "I'm sorry, I thought—"

Young interrupted him with a hiss. "You don't think. You do what I tell you to do. This is a warning, Stan. This matter must be handled delicately and if you do not have the discretion we require, then you will be dealt with." Young got up from the table, then turned back to Stan, his face pleasant and professional again.

"If we are clear? I'll see you at our offices this evening, seven o'clock sharp. Make certain Ms. Madsen has what she needs for that meeting before you come."

Young left Stan sitting in the booth. When he was out of sight, Stan pulled out his handkerchief and wiped the cold sweat from his brow.

Chapter 9

"I'm sorry, Toni. If I could take it for you, you know I would. Miguel has never done this before, you know he is reliable."

"I don't want to hear 'reliable,' okay? Where is he then? I'm supposed to be back in the States today—and now I'm delayed two days because of his incompetence. I want his ass, Larry. And I'll want yours if this ever happens again. Understand?"

Toni sat back in her chair with an irritated sigh and adjusted her sunglasses as she looked around the square. There were several people gathered at the far side, taking out instruments and talking with animated gestures. Toni nodded in their direction.

"What's going on over there?"

Larry followed her glance and shrugged. That is the *Bateria*, uh…the percussion group for *Grêmio Recreativo Escol de Samba*[1] *Caix. Festa da Ribeira Pituba* is in a few days. We are about to be treated to a real *Batucada*—they are one of the best schools in the area."

1. Creative Samba School Group. All samba schools in Brazil, and many around the world, start with the abbreviation G.R.E.S. to officially mark themselves as legitimate samba schools.

Toni shielded her eyes as she watched a pretty girl in a bright skirt twirl to the laughter of the others. Toni turned back to Larry. "What the devil is a 'batacuda'? Jeez, didn't they have a festival last week?"

Larry laughed. "A 'batacuda' is a—how do you say it—a jam session. That girl, I think is the *Passista*². I've seen her before, she is very good."

"Hmph." Toni pushed back her chair and stood. "Well, enjoy. I have to get out of here if I am going to make my flight tomorrow evening." She picked up the briefcase that sat on the ground beside her.

Larry grabbed her arm. "Wait. There is another matter we need to discuss."

Toni rolled her eyes as she sat again. "What."

Larry paused, and the sound of a *cavaquinho*³ being tuned floated over them. "It's about Jorge."

"Sheesh, Larry. I left you in charge here so I could take care of other matters. What about Jorge? And this better be good."

Larry leaned in closer to Toni. "I tried, Toni, you know I did. It seems that on Jorge's last flight, forty thousand dollars went missing. Believe me, I worked him over, but he claims he knows nothing about it. The House says they want him out. The plan was to have Miguel take him out on this run. No Miguel. But it has to be done. Orders from the very top."

Toni sat back again, taking her hat off and tossing it on the table. "I can't believe this. Do you know how much is at risk here? Not just the money, Larry. I can't afford to be involved in any *hint* of conflict down here. How am I supposed to do this, can you answer that? That's why we hire idiots like Miguel."

Larry put his hand up. "Calm down. I've worked it out." He put his backpack on the table and opened it, pulling out a slim case and several books. "Put these in your bag."

2. A girl solo dancer who is younger and unmarried (symbolically). She is chosen for her excellent skills in dancing to the samba beat of the bateria, She dances in the samba parade, accompanied by male dancers playing their pandeiros, or tambourine.

3. A small 4-stringed instrument used in samba music. Originating in Portugal, it also was the inspiration for the ukulele.

Toni picked up one of the books. It was a helicopter manual. "What am I supposed to do with this? Throw Jorge out of the helicopter and fly myself back to Salvador?" She tossed the book back on the table.

"Of course not, Toni. You should know me better than that by now. Have I ever let you down?"

Toni scowled at him. "This is not the time to ask me a question like that, now is it Larry?"

Larry laughed again. "You're right." He sobered and continued. "These books are the manuals for the fleet of helicopters at Bolatti's airstrip in Ilhéus. You are guaranteed that no witnesses will see you there. I have hi-lighted the sections in each that you'll need. Simply attach the small device to the bird. It will cause a very real-looking smoke fire. Jorge will bring the bird down for an emergency landing, and I will be there. *I* will take Jorge out, and you will get into São Paulo in time for a leisurely lunch before your flight."

Toni picked up the book again. "And how will I know when to do this—without blowing myself up?"

"About half way through your trip, you'll go over some mountains. There is a map in the bag, which has the landmark you will use to gauge location, circled. When you see it, get that device in place. All the details are in this case, along with the device and a few tools you'll need." Larry took Toni's hand. "It'll be a breeze. Believe me."

Toni stuffed the books and case into her bag reluctantly. "Well, I *don't* believe you. But I have no choice, do I?" Toni stood.

"This better work, Larry, or you'll have me to answer to. Understand?" Toni picked up the briefcase again, and then smiled as she leaned over and caressed Larry's jaw. "But if it *does* work, we will be too busy celebrating for lunch. I've gotta go."

Several women walked by, carrying their *destaque*, and the bright colors, beading and feathers of their elaborate carnival costumes distracted Toni for a moment. When they passed, Toni turned back to Larry.

"Just you don't get caught up in the festivities here and miss our rendezvous, buddy, or I'll use your balls as my *agogô*[4] at the next Carnaval. Now let me get my sweet, American tourist self out to Ilhéus."

4. A cow-bell sounding instrument with two bells that are struck by a wooden stick. The bells can also produce a sound by squeezing them so that they strike each other.

Chapter 10

Toni stood at the entrance of the hangar, as her eyes adjusted to the shadowy interior. She spotted a heavy set man smoking a cigar, and headed in his direction.

"Excuse me, do you speak English?"

Sabo turned and looked at the gringo woman approaching him. She was what Bahians called a mulatta. She tall, beautiful and full-bodied. He smiled appreciatively at her long, well-toned legs, the beads of sweat above her rounded, full breasts, and wondered if her skin tasted salty. Like most American tourists visiting 'the wilds' of Brazil, she wore an expensive safari outfit, khaki shorts and matching top. Her hair was mostly tucked under a white NY Yankees baseball cap, but a few strands had escaped and clung to her damp neck. Also, she wore the boots the tourists favored, hiking boots, they called them. Sabo chuckled. Two hours walking in them and their feet would be blistered.

He headed towards her. "Yes, senhora. Welcome to Sabo Airlines. How can I assist you?"

"I want to hire a helicopter, right away. Jorge Mantegna was recommended to me"

Sabo shrugged apologetically. "I am afraid he is not available. He is on a job right now and not expected back until Tuesday next. But no need to worry, here at Sabo Airline, we live to serve you."

Sabo smiled at the woman, revealing his tobacco-stained teeth. "Where do you need to go? I can get you a pilot first thing in the morning."

"No. You don't understand. I have to leave Ilhéus today. Now. My tour group leaves tomorrow from Salvador and I can't miss that flight."

With a look of concern, Sabo wheezed, "Senhora, that is not within my power. You see, all of my pilots are on missions today."

Sabo saw his mechanic strolling outside the hangar and yelled angrily, "Antonio, You get back over here and finish number 24, rapido, rapido!!"

The young man ignored him, and continued to stroll towards the airfield. Sabo turned to Toni. "Excuse me, senhora. These lazy idiots. I will be right back."

Toni grabbed his arm. "Look, I have to get out of here—tonight."

Sabo watched the retreating form of Antonio and turned to Toni. "I am sorry, it is out of my control. If you will excuse me." He hurried out of the hangar, yelling and cursing at Antonio's back.

"Get back to your duties, before I throw you out on your ear, you lazy donkey!"

Antonio turned to Sabo. "Mark is about to land."

Sabo poked his chubby finger into Antonio's chest and scanned the sky. "You idiot! There is no helo up there. Can't you see? No one radioed. He is not on the radar."

Suddenly, a helicopter appeared, approaching low and sweeping over their heads. Sabo lost his footing and fell into the dust. He got up, cursing, "Yankee jackass!"

The helicopter banked and made a smooth, rolling landing. Antonio ran towards it as Toni came up to Sabo, who was brushing the dirt from his clothes.

"What about him? Can he take me to Salvador?"

Sabo spit in the dust. "No. You don't want him. He is irresponsible."

Toni dug around in her bag. "Look, if he can fly me there, I'll take my chances."

Sabo glared once more at the figure lighting from the helicopter and headed back for the hangar. Toni stopped him, flashing a thick wad of bills in front of him.

"Look, money is no object. I have to get out of here immediately and I want him to take me."

Sabo's eyes widened with greed as he stared at the wad of bills in the woman's hand. Licking his lips, he said in his most ingratiating tone of voice, "Well, senhora. If it is so important, I hate to see a beautiful lady in distress. But I must warn you, this character is very low. Maybe if you were to give me something to show him?"

Toni peeled off several bills, which Sabo grabbed hastily. "I will see what I can do. Um momento." Sabo moved swiftly to the hangar, where Mark had just disappeared. As soon as he was out of Toni's sight, his tone changed.

"What are you doing here? You were supposed to be in Salvador tonight. You are destroying my business!"

Mark looked up from the magazine he was scanning. "You got your days mixed up, partner. Seems the folks in Salvador needed a pick up last Thursday."

"Impossible." Sabo sputtered. "Anyway, it doesn't matter. They are imbeciles. You will get ready to fly the lady to Salvador right away."

Mark tossed the magazine aside. "Not me."

Sabo slammed his hand on the desk in disgust. "It is very important that she get to Salvador tonight and you will fly her."

Mark brushed by Sabo and got some water. "Not tonight I won't."

"One day you will crash and burn, and that will be a happy day for all." He followed Mark, his voice now wheedling. "She will pay big money. Money is no object."

Mark took a long swallow, then poured the rest of the water over his head. "Is that so? Well, I don't do druggies. You know that, so don't ask."

"You idiot. She is not a druggie, she—"

Just then, Toni entered the hangar. Mark lowered his sunglasses on his nose to get a better look. He smiled lazily and whispered to Sabo, "Never could resist a nice pair of calves."

• • •

Toni felt her stomach lurch as the Bell UH-1 helicopter climbed up into the sky. She swallowed and closed her eyes to steady herself. Then she turned deliberately to Mark.

"Mark Davis. So, you're American, right? Have you been in Brazil long?"

Mark made a few adjustments on the board and then answered, "Why?"

"Just making conversation. Don't worry, I won't turn you in."

Mark laughed. "Turn me in? Thanks for the compliment. The flying ex-con. Do I fit the stereotype?"

Toni looked away. "I didn't mean it like that."

"Sure you did. One out of every four gringos living down here is a con, or running away from somebody or something."

"And you? What are you running away from?"

Mark didn't answer. Toni changed the subject. "How long will it take to get to Salvador?"

"About twenty-six minutes. Just over the Maracas mountains." He turned to her. "Now it is my turn to ask questions. Why is a savvy Midwestern lady flying back door into Salvador?"

"I'm on an adventure tour of Brazil."

Mark looked at her. "Right. Well, you can't get more adventurous than flying Sabo Airlines. This piece of shit may or may not get us over there."

Toni gripped the edges of her seat. "What?!"

Mark grinned. "Oh, Sabo didn't tell you? This piece of crap has a busted chip detector, among other things. That's why yours truly was paid in advance."

Suddenly, there was a loud bang and the helicopter dropped altitude. Toni grabbed Mark's leg. Enjoying her fear, Mark pretended to lose control of the aircraft for a moment. Toni screamed as Mark steadied the helicopter. He put his hand on her thigh.

"It's cool, just a compressor stall. Relax."

"Relax? You put me in this junk heap and risk my life for a measly $2,000.00?"

Mark looked sharply at her. "Two thousand?" He shook his head and smiled.

"The great Sabo does it again. Lady, you just got beat."

"What?"

Mark chuckled. "Sabo paid me $500.00 and charged you two thousand. He'll write it off as a government mission and charge Brasilia $1,600. Well, anyway, that's the way it goes. Who's picking you up in Salvador?"

Toni looked straight ahead. "That's no concern of yours."

Mark's brows furrowed with irritation. "Look, let's cut the bullshit. You're here to drop dope cash, aren't you? That's how most bush pilots make their living here—but not me. Lady, I've been around long enough to know a fake when I see one."

Toni turned to him. "Oh really? Then why now?"

"Because you don't fit the mold. There's something about you that says 'I'm too stupid to know what's gonna happen to me.' This is your first time in the country, isn't it? You ask too many questions and the only thing you're not wearing that says 'American' is a Coach bag."

Toni turned away, glancing quickly at her Coach key chain. "I beg your pardon, but these clothes are very international."

Mark laughed out loud. "Yeah, right. Let me guess. Banana Republic, Water Tower Mall, Chicago."

Toni continued staring out of the window and said nothing. She saw a large lake, the mountain range looming dark behind it. "It's beautiful here. What's this area called?"

"The Highlands."

Suddenly, her beeper chirped. Toni reached for her bag. "Look, I'm getting a little air sick. Do you mind if I lie down in the back? Maybe if I don't have to look down, my stomach will settle."

Mark smiled at her, "Sure. I'm sorry I can't join you."

Toni ignored him and climbed unsteadily to the back seat. She sat behind Mark, out of eyeshot, and put her legs up on the seat and pretended to settle in. Then she opened her bag and flipped through several tech manuals which listed the internal plans for various helicopters. When she got to the Bell UH-1, she went to the page on it's internal wiring. She pulled out a small box of instruments, and adjusted a valve from the helo bay to a small device. Then she attached the black box and put the book and instruments back into her bag.

A few seconds later, there was a small explosion. Black smoke poured out of the box and the helicopter shuddered. Toni jumped up, screaming.

"There's a fire! Oh my god! There's a fire back here!"

She climbed into the cockpit, hysterical. "Get me out of here! Get me out!!"

"Oh shit." Mark cursed as the smoke filled the cabin.

Mark began emergency landing procedures as the helicopter's gauges spun wildly out of control. He banked the helicopter right as it rapidly descended towards the dark jungle below. "Strap in. I'm looking for an open area to land."

He picked up the radio and shouted above the noise, "Mayday, mayday. This is TA-56. TA-56 going down 15 NNW, Burieta."

Mark turned the helicopter towards an open area. As the helicopter touched down, a man ran from the thick brush, pointing a submachine gun at Mark. Another man opened the passenger door and jerked Toni out of the cab. As a third man opened fire on the helicopter, Mark reached over to grab Toni, but was only able to get her bag, as the helicopter went up and banked left in an effort to evade gunfire.

As he brought the helicopter around again to go after Toni, Mark pulled an automatic rifle from behind the passenger seat.

"Alright fellahs, let's get this party started."

Suddenly, there was a loud bang and the helicopter spun out of control. Mark was thrown against the door as fire erupted in the cockpit. Down below, the three men and Toni watched the helicopter disappear over the palm tree line. A moment later, there was a crash and explosion. As the flames leapt into the dark skies, Toni and the men climbed into a jeep and drove off into the jungle.

Chapter 11

Beverly kicked her shoes off as she entered the apartment. Dropping her briefcase on the couch, she padded into the kitchen and poured a glass of water. The clock on the microwave glowed 5:15 P.M. She had forty-five minutes to shower and get over to the Zanzibar Blue to meet Dexter.

Her heart was pounding in her chest, and she wasn't sure if it was excitement over seeing Dexter again, or fear of what he might have found out about Mark. She looked at her glass and then poured the water down the drain. She needed a drink. Taking a bottle of sherry from the cupboard, she was just pouring it into the glass, when her apartment door opened and Lauri burst in.

"If you are making drinks, I want one too. What are you drinking?" Lauri slammed the door behind her and came into the kitchen.

Beverly poured another glass for Lauri and then sat on the stool beside her. Lauri put her hand on Beverly's arm and asked gently, "So? How are you doing? Did you find out anything?"

Beverly sipped her drink and shook her head, no. "But I'm having dinner with Dexter tonight. Maybe he's found something out."

Lauri's mouth dropped open. "You are having *dinner* with Dexter? I thought he lived in D.C. or something."

"He does. But he had to come in for business this afternoon, so we're having dinner."

Lauri tapped her glass, frowning. "I don't know sis. It seems pretty suspicious to me that you call him in distress, and he just *happens* to be coming to Philly in time for dinner."

Beverly stood up. "Lauri, I am not in the mood. It isn't suspicious, frankly, I think it was lucky *and* damned nice of him, considering we haven't talked in two years." She put her drink on the counter and sighed. "Besides, it's not like that. Dexter is like a brother to me."

Lauri snickered. "Yeah right, tell me all about it. *You* may think of him as a brother, but I can tell you, he does not think of you the same way. You are asking for it."

Beverly slammed her hand on the counter. Her eyes filling with tears, she yelled angrily at Lauri, "Stop it! I don't want to hear your insinuations, okay? Mark is missing and Dexter has offered to help me find him. The wedding is in a few weeks, Lauri, and I have no idea if Mark is even going to be there. No one else will tell me what's going on, Mark hasn't, and his mother won't. If Dexter can find out for me, then dammit, I'll have dinner with him—or anything else I want to find out. And I don't want to hear another word about it from you!"

Beverly stormed out of the kitchen and slammed the door to her bedroom. A second later, Lauri heard the shower running.

Twenty minutes later, Beverly came out of the bedroom. She had changed into a pair of black slacks and an oversized, white silk shirt. Her makeup was freshly applied, though it didn't completely cover the puffiness around her eyes. Lauri was sitting on the sofa.

"I'm sorry, Bev. I know you're scared and worried. Sometimes I let my big mouth get in the way. I think it's great that Dexter will be there for you, and I hope he can tell you the deal on Mark. I hate seeing you like this." Lauri got up and gave Beverly a hug. Pulling away slightly, she grinned.

"Besides, we've already paid for those dresses. What am I supposed to do with that flouncy coral thing?" She watched until Beverly smiled slightly, then laughed a little too. "Do you forgive me? You know I love you."

"I do. But you're wrong about Dex. Sure, we spent some time together, but it was a long time ago. He knows the deal, and he respects it. Okay?"

"Okay. What time are you meeting him?"

"Seven. At Zanzibar Blue."

Lauri pushed Beverly gently to the sofa. "Then we have time to finish our drinks, right? Of course, this is my third."

Beverly's eyebrows raised in surprise.

"Well, I had to do something while I waited for you to come out so I could grovel and beg forgiveness!"

• • •

Dexter watched the door from the bar. He saw Beverly walk in, and his heart lurched at the thought of what he'd lost. She was as beautiful as ever. It was as if time stood still for her. Dexter watched her ginger-lipsticked lips form a question of the maitre'd, saw the veins in her neck pulse as she scanned the seated diners for his face, and remembered how her skin tasted on his lips. He shook himself. "Maintain, brother," he muttered to himself, "get it together, she is someone else's woman."

He stood and brushed his jacket off. As he walked towards her, he reminded himself that he was there as a friend. A friend with information that she was not going to be too happy about. This was not about him. It was about her. And Mark. The man she loved.

"Beverly."

She turned at the familiar voice, and smiled. Hugging him, she murmured, "Dexter, it's been a long time."

They separated, and Dexter looked into her eyes, then away. *Maintain*, he reminded himself. He looked up at her again and smiled. "You look wonderful, as usual. Why don't we go in? I've reserved a table."

• • •

"Apparently, he's been out of the Navy since last December." Dexter pushed his plate aside.

"Why didn't he tell me that? What has he been doing since then? I...I just don't understand. Only a month ago, the last time I saw him, he told me he was going on a mission with his squadron. Why did he lie to me?"

Dexter fought the anger at Mark surging up in him as he watched Beverly's suffering. How could he have done it? He had everything Dexter had ever loved, and he threw it away. Just threw it away. He took a deep breath, and with a steady voice, asked quietly, "Bev, what do you want me to do? Do you want me to find him? Talk to him?"

Beverly felt numb all over. She didn't know if she wanted to run, or scream or faint. She dug her nails into her palms until she felt composed. With eyes filled with shock and hurt, she whispered to herself, "What did I do wrong?" She looked up at Dexter, "I just don't understand why he would just walk away. How can I deal with this, if I don't know what I did wrong?"

Dexter took her hands in his and squeezed them. "Beverly. You didn't do anything wrong. You know Mark, he's always been hot tempered and impetuous. But he loves you. If he disappeared, there has to be a good reason why. I'll do what I can to find out, okay?"

Beverly pulled her hands away and stood abruptly. Reaching for her bag, she said, "I...I need to get out of here, okay? Thanks, Dex. For everything."

Dexter stood too. "Do you want me to take you home?"

Beverly backed away from the table. "No. I need to be alone. I have to think...about this. I'm sorry." With that she turned and ran out of the restaurant.

Dexter sat heavily. "Damn you, Mark." He signaled for the waiter. "Bring me the check."

Chapter 12

Dexter Racine stood at the doors of his clothes closet, an immaculate A-shirt tucked into his blue and white pinstriped boxer shorts. Black, wavy hairs curled from the top of his undershirt, and matched the wavy, biweekly trimmed hair brushed neatly back from his face. His dark brows were knitted over heavy lidded, clear hazel eyes in a combination of irritation and nearsightedness. He looked at the row of blue and black suits, the starched white shirts still on cleaners' hangers.

"Not one blue shirt," he muttered.

He turned his attention to the rack of silk ties hanging on the door. They too were in muted shades of black or blue, with an occasional drop of color in a conservative paisley or striped print. His shoes were neatly lined up on the carpeted floor of his closet, all buffed and shined, all lace up—buckles were not regulation in his office. Not for the first time that week, Dexter wondered what would happen if he decided to wear a pair of loafers to the office. That was, if he had loafers.

He looked at his watch. It was getting late and he had a briefing on a new case at 9:00 A.M. Pulling out a blue suit and white shirt, Dexter got dressed. With a final polish of his "flashy" gold wire-rimmed glasses, he

adjusted them on his nose, picked up his briefcase and slammed the front
door behind him.

• • •

As Dexter inched through the morning rush hour traffic of the
Baltimore-Washington Parkway, he allowed his thoughts to stray to
Beverly Madsen.

Until yesterday, almost two years had passed since he had spoken to her.
Two years since she had told him she was going to marry Mark Davis, his
best friend. Beverly. His former girlfriend who he, unfortunately, still loved.
He quickly pushed that thought away and focused, instead, on Mark.

Mark Davis. In college, they'd called him "Belafonte," he was so
smooth. Mark had only three goals in life back then: flying, making money
and pleasing women while flying and making money. He had certainly
perfected the pleasing women part in college, Dexter thought ruefully. I
never should have let him meet Beverly.

He knew Mark had not taken Beverly from him, but that didn't make
it any easier to accept. Women had always flocked to Mark for attention,
and to Dexter for advice. That was just the way it was.

They'd served together as officers in the Navy, and they had both
believed that it was their destiny to be great leaders. They'd save the world
and then go home to their women until the next crisis, and off they'd go
again. Dexter just hadn't known that his girl would end up Mark's wife at
the end of the story.

And now, on the eve of the wedding Dexter had hoped would be his,
Mark was missing. Out of the past came Beverly again and, Dexter
thought ruefully, he had to find out what had happened to the man who
was marrying the only woman Dexter would ever love.

Dexter flashed his I.D. card at the security gate and parked his car. As
he walked into the building, he thought about how funny life was. Mark
was flying, traveling the world and had his woman. Dexter had a desk job,

in a room with no windows. He had some excitement, but little money and no Beverly.

Dexter entered the building that housed the U.S. Secret Service Headquarters. Checking his watch, he decided to take the short cut through the main briefing room to his office. The center was buzzing with activity. Special Agent Johanson approached him and handed him a report.

"Good morning, sir. This is the Chicago debrief, sir."

"Good work." Dexter took the report into his office and closed the door. A second later, there was a knock on the door. Agent Davits walked in and handed him another file.

"Sir, FBI's last report on Tennison was April 2nd. If he were still in Boston, he certainly wouldn't have hung around later than the 3rd."

Dexter opened the file, scanning it quickly. "Did 47 or Providence have any success?"

Davits looked down at his shoes. "Uh, I don't know, sir. I didn't check."

Dexter didn't look up from the report. "Didn't check."

"No, sir."

Dexter closed the file and handed it back to Davits. "Mr. Davits, finish your investigation properly. I don't have the time or energy to waste listening to incomplete headword. I want to know where Tennison is, stat."

"Yes, sir." As Davits turned to leave, Special Agent Bremmer walked in.

"Damn, Dex, that boy looks like you whacked his pee pee."

Dexter leaned back in his chair. "Yeah, well gotta stop these neophytes from taking the easy way out. Otherwise, they'll end up like you."

Bremmer sat down. "Yeah," he sighed, "your girlfriend told me the same thing last night. Listen, some heads rolled this morning. Take a look at this." He tossed a photograph on the desk in front of Dexter.

Dexter picked up the photograph and shook his head. "John Tanaka. What is he doing back in town? I thought they extradited him back in 87."

"So did I. But he's back and getting very cozy with the Michigan Lt. Governor Richard Chase. You know, they are having a mud fight up there this election."

"Did Albans reopen this?"

"Nope. Not this time. The situation is too sensitive right now. I want this sonofabitch. But we can't touch him unless we have hard proof.

"So, you want me to take it?" Dexter dropped the photograph back on the desk.

"It's over my pay grade, Dex. Besides, you can't handle your load now."

"What? If I hadn't saved your—" The phone rang. "Excuse me, I'll finish with you in a second."

"Special Projects. Dexter Racine. Mrs. Davis? How are you? What? Why was he in Brazil? Mrs. Davis…don't worry. I'll take care of it. Yes. I'll get right down there. Let me jot your number down. Mrs. Davis…Mrs. Davis—everything will be fine. I'll call you as soon as I get there, alright? Okay, you too. Good bye." Dexter hung up the phone slowly.

"Bad news?"

Dexter rubbed his eyes and looked at Bremmer. "I can't believe it. Mark is dead."

Your friend the helo pilot?"

"Yeah. Apparently his helo crashed in Brazil."

"Brazil? What's he doing down there?"

"Who knows? Mark is always somewhere he shouldn't be. That was his mother. She wants me to bring the body back."

"When's the last time you talked to him."

"It's been a while." Dexter stood abruptly. "Look, I'm gonna have to get down there. Can you cover for me for a few days?"

"No problem Dex. Hey, I'm sorry."

Dexter squeezed Bremmer's shoulder. "Yeah. Me too. I just had dinner with his fiancée' last night, and now I might have to tell her that the wedding is being replaced by a funeral. Can you believe this?"

Chapter 13

"We settled the property on the 12th, so you should see a statement by the 14th, 15th latest…Manhattan Trust, $1,480,044.00…right…No problem, Mr. Harris. Of course, it's our pleasure. If you have any other questions or concerns, just give me a call and if I'm not in the office, just have me paged. Okay then, take care. Goodbye."

Beverly hung up the phone and rested her face in her hands. She was having a hard time concentrating on her work. Last night's meeting with Dexter kept running through her head. Mark had been out of the military, and had never told her. That last night together, so tender and loving, all lies. He'd looked right into her eyes and lied. Made love to her, knowing all the while he was leaving.

She searched her mind over and over for hints that she'd never seen. How could she not have known? Of course, she knew he'd been upset over that mission that had gone wrong months ago. She'd spent a lot of nights with him, holding him, listening to his anger, his pain and disillusionment But he'd never said it had ended with his dismissal from service. *Maybe,* Beverly thought, *everything was a lie. Maybe he never intended to marry me. Maybe he never really even loved me.*

She thought back to the years in college, when she had been Dexter's girl and Mark's friend. Mark had every girl on campus after him, even she had been attracted. She remembered wondering how two men, as different as Dexter and Mark were from each other, had been such good friends. Dexter did not take part in Mark's escapades with women, he was happy having her as his girl. Even after they broke up, Dexter didn't take advantage of all the girls who were attracted to his hazel-eyed, soft-spoken charm. Oh, he'd dated of course, but he didn't run the way Mark had. The only girl who Mark had never had, was her.

Beverly shook her head angrily. Maybe that was what this was all about. Maybe Mark had gone after her, because she was the only girl he thought he couldn't have. She stood and paced angrily around her office. How could she have been such a fool?

She sat again, heavily. But she did love him. It was that simple. And he had treated her like a queen. Surely he had loved her too? It couldn't have *all* been lies. Beverly didn't know what to think, or what to do. And now Mark was gone, their wedding was probably never going to happen, and unless Dexter found him, she'd probably never get the chance to ask him why.

The phone rang, interrupting her thoughts. Taking a breath, Beverly sat up in her chair and picked up the receiver. "Beverly Madsen, may I help you?"

"Dr. Reisling, what a surprise! How good to hear from you! Yes, of course, Michael. And how is Doris?…Good, good. What can I do for you, Dr. Re—uh—Michael?"

Beverly picked up a pen and started doodling. "Why yes, we are the sponsors of Columbia Village…well, I don't know…I'm not assigned to that project, but I can put you in touch with my associate, Stan Towers. I'm sure he'll be able to assist you…well, of course, if you'd like me to. I'll give him a call and then get back to you, okay? Yes, I'd like that too. We'll make a date really soon. Best to Doris…I'll talk to you later. Okay. Goodbye."

Beverly tossed the pen aside and pressed Stan's intercom.

"Stan."

"It's Beverly. Are you busy?"

Beverly could hear Stan adjusting the phone on his ear, the fabric of his suit rustled through the receiver.

"I'm never too busy for you Beverly. What's up?"

"I just got a call from an old friend of mine who is interested in buying into Columbia and…"

Stan interrupted her. "Bev, that development has been booked for two years. People are crawling out of the woodwork trying to get in."

Beverly tapped her fingers impatiently. "Come on, Stan. We both know you could help him out if you wanted to."

Stan smiled into the phone. "Well, that's true, Bev. *If* I wanted to. Of course, if you were on the team, *you'd* be able to help him yourself."

"Come on Stan, don't do this. I am considering it. And you know, doing me this tiny favor—of at least looking into it, would go a long way towards building good will between…business partners?"

"Okay, okay. You know you're taking advantage of the soft spot in my heart for you, don't you Bev?"

"Oh Stan, I might believe that, if I didn't already know you don't have a heart." She laughed. "I'll owe you big."

"That you will, Bev. That you will. What's his name?"

"Michael Reisling, he was one of my professors at Florida A&M, but he's at Penn now."

"Someone's at my door, Bev. Let me get back to you in a few."

Stan hung up the phone and turned to his computer. He did a search of the University of Pennsylvania's faculty roster. After finding Reisling's name and status, he switched to another program and entered the information. The screen blinked for a moment and then a profile appeared.

Dr. Michael Bobby Reisling, III

Yale Ph.D./Economics

Debt Ratio: 42, Medical History: 4,56,2B Est. life term: May 2026

Annual Income: $105,000.00

Element Assignment: University Professor

Stan got up and locked his office door. He walked over to his wall safe and removed two CD-ROMs labeled "COLONNADE," and went back to his desk, inserting the first one into the computer. The program requested an access code and password. He entered the information and then sat back as the database reviewed Reisling's profile. Reisling's name came up on the approved roster. Stan leaned forward and reviewed the paragraph beneath Reisling's name.

Settle lien #34582 Sovereign Bank for property lot 59 Rittenhouse Square Bank approval 565779, Misawa Bank.

Approval granted $575,000.00. Settle all loans at 4%. Signature not to exceed $135,000.00. Enter into action Y (Yes) N (No).

Stan hit the Y key. The screen displayed:

Element assigned unit/lot 7B, 472 Wuthering Heights Drive, Columbia Village.

Stan leaned back in his chair and smiled. Then, he popped out the first CD and put in the second, downloading the file to it. After putting both discs back into the safe, he called Beverly.

"I will expect you to be at your sharpest and most charming in Detroit, Ms. Madsen. I will expect you to work your magic and have them falling all over themselves to get you on board. *And* I expect a 5% cut on your sign-on bonus. If you agree to all of the above, I can get your friend a place at Columbia. Agreed?"

"Ah, Stan, you drive a hard bargain, but I guess that's why you are one of the best. You got it, you snake."

"Good. Then have Reisling meet us out at Columbia tomorrow morning. We can show him the site before we head out to the airport."

"Will do. Thanks, Stan."

"Sure, sure. Just make sure you wear that sweet, gray suit of yours. You look stunning in it."

Chapter 14

Dexter arrived in Ilhéus just after dawn the following morning. He drove
down the narrow but busy Ilhéus-Olivenga Road. The streets were filled
with women carrying baskets of fresh produce and fruit, children playing
soccer in the dusty square, old men sitting in the open air café drinking
strong but smooth Brazilian coffee. He pulled over in front of a stucco
building which was once, he thought, pink, though there were only flakes
of peeling, faded paint on its façade.

He turned off the ignition and sat for a moment, closing his burning
eyes, and then squinted to make out the number on the front of the building. Shrugging, he got out of the car. If it wasn't the right place, someone
would be able to direct him. Grabbing his bag, he slammed the door and
climbed the stairs. An old women was standing at a makeshift fruit stand
on the corner. He smiled and nodded his head at her, but she just stared
at him suspiciously, then turned back to her wares. Friendly place.

It was cool in the lobby. Old furniture, shabby, though meticulously
repaired was arranged haphazardly around the small room. Against the far
wall was the check in desk, and behind it stood an old man organizing

papers. A younger women stood behind him, sorting envelopes. Neither looked up as he approached them.

"*Com licenca por favor. Voce fala Ingles?*"

The old man looked up and glanced at the younger woman, who remained silent. "Yes, a little. How can I help you?"

"My name is Dexter Racine. I was a friend of an American that lived here, Mark Davis?"

The old man nodded, "Ah, yes. The famoso piloto."

Dexter grinned, "Yes. You could call him that. I came to pick up his things."

The old man clasped his hands together and bowed his head. "Senhor, I am very sorry to hear about the death of your amigo. May St. Peter bless his soul." He crossed himself.

"Thank you. Would you please show me his room?"

The old man shook his head. "That will not be possible. Mr. Davis was not the best of tenants. His bill must be paid before I can permit his personal items to be taken."

Dexter was astounded. "Bill? What kind of place is this? The man is dead." Exasperated, he shook his head. "How much did he owe you?"

"Three hundred American dollars."

"Three hund—I don't believe this." Dexter pulled out his wallet and peeled off some bills, slapping them on the counter. "Fine. Now will you take me to his room?"

The young woman came out from behind the counter. "He lived in one of our cottages out back. Very private. Please follow."

They walked out a side door and down a small, dirt path. Dexter followed close behind, admiring the woman's small waist and swinging hips.

They stopped in front of a dilapidated shack. The woman stopped and pulled a key from her skirt pocket. As she put the key into the lock, she asked, "Did you know him long?"

"He was a close friend for many years," Dexter answered, taking note of her protective tone of voice.

She stepped aside and allowed Dexter to enter the cottage. It was bare, but neat. Mark's memorabilia decorated the room. Dexter picked up a photograph of the two of them, taken their senior year at college. They were wearing their fraternity colors, arms thrown around each other, laughing. He put the picture down and turned to the woman.

"This is a beautiful little town, Miss—"

"Caterina."

"Caterina. And a beautiful name." He glanced at her wrist and noticed her wearing Mark's father's watch. "How long were you involved with Mark, Caterina?"

Surprised, Caterina and stepped away from Dexter. She looked out of the window and as she answered softly, "Our hearts were one."

Dexter turned and sat on the edge of the bed. He looked up at Caterina, suddenly exhausted. "Do you know what happened to him? Can you help me find him—find out what happened to him, Caterina?"

Caterina took a couple of cautious steps towards Dexter, then stopped. "He worked for Sabo Bolatti, down at the airstrip. Perhaps he can tell you what happened."

Dexter got up from the bed, and walked to the door. "Thank you. I will come back and pack his things." He walked out of the cottage.

Caterina came out after him. "Wait. I will go with you."

Dexter turned and looked at the woman. "That won't be necessary. I can speak a little Portuguese."

Caterina put her hand on Dexter's arm. "Please. I, too, want to know what happened to Mark." Her large dark eyes, implored him, "Please."

Dexter hesitated, and then nodded assent. "Let's go. My Jeep is just out front."

• • •

Dexter pulled up in front of the hangar and hopped out, going around the other side of the car to assist Caterina. She shook her head at him. "No, I will wait here for you."

Dexter shrugged, "As you wish. I'll be right back." He turned and walked into the building.

Sabo was on the phone. He waved Dexter over and motioned for him to sit. When he hung up, he put on a wide smile and shook Dexter's hand. "Welcome to Sabo Airlines, Senhor. How can I assist you?"

"My name is Dexter Racine. I was a friend of one of your pilots, Mark Davis."

Sabo's smile faded quickly. "Yes. Mr. Davis. A most ungrateful pilot, at best. It is sad what happened to him, but I am afraid it was due to his own negligence."

"Pardon me?"

"Yes. It is not right to speak ill of the dead, but he was very headstrong. You must understand, in Brazil many foreigners are desperados." Sabo rushed on, "This is not to say Senhor Davis was one, but he lacked much courage and was constantly surrounded by controversy. At any rate, he, as many American bush pilots do, ferried parcels and passengers around the great Amazon. Sometimes, my weaker pilots succumbed to the money offered by drug lords to fly missions of death. I, of course, highly discourage this behavior, but as I said, Senhor Davis was headstrong and greedy. He was killed flying a drug mission, which I knew nothing about. He crashed in the highlands.

Dexter sat back in his chair. "Were there any survivors?"

Sabo shook his head sadly. "No. He flew alone. As I said, it was most tragic. He destroyed my most expensive helicopter. Very, very tragic for my business."

"And his remains?"

"Remains. There were no remains, Senhor. Just a fiery crash of destruction by a foolish, headstrong man and great damage to property." Sabo looked past Dexter at the entrance, "May I help you Senhora?"

Dexter turned and saw Caterina standing in the shadows. He stood. "She's with me. Thank you for your help Senhor Sabo."

Sabo stuffed his cigar in his mouth and stood too. "If there is some way I can be of help, please feel free to contact me. Of course I know nothing, but…how long will you be in Ilhéus, Senhor?"

"Until Thursday. If you think of anything else, I can be reached at—" Caterina answered, "exchange 567."

Sabo nodded. "Very well. I will certainly do so, yes. It is always a sad time when a soul and an expensive helicopter are lost."

Dexter took a couple of steps and then turned. "Senhor, one more thing. Did Mark file a flight plan?"

Sabo made a show of shuffling papers and did not look up as he stuttered, "I am not sure, as I said, he was dealing with very shady people and I knew nothing of his trip. No. I am sure he did not."

"Well, thank you. Good bye." Dexter took Caterina's arm and they walked back to the car.

Caterina whispered, "He's lying. Mark would never fly for the drug lords."

Dexter replied, "I know. Maybe someone around here really knows what happened?"

"Perhaps." Caterina climbed into the car and waited until Dexter was in as well before she continued. "I spoke to that mechanic," she nodded her head towards the side of the hangar, where a young boy leaned against it, studiously looking the other way. "He gave me a note. He wants us to meet him in the favela tonight."

Dexter turned the ignition on the car and backed up. As he switched gears, he said, "Caterina, thank you for your help, but I'd better take it from here."

Caterina laughed scornfully, "You'll take it from here? And how will you find the favela?"

Dexter started driving. "It might not be safe for a woman."

Caterina looked at him hard, "It is no place for an arrogant American, Senhor. You do not speak the language, do not know the contact—do not even know where the favela is. Perhaps I should take it from here?"

Dexter pulled the car to the side of the road and parked. Then he turned to her. "Look, I didn't mean it like that. It's just that it could be dangerous. Obviously Mark cared about you. You're wearing his watch. His father gave him that watch when he started flying as a boy. It meant everything to him, and he gave it to you. If you meant that much to him, I just don't want to see you hurt."

Caterina relaxed, her voice wistful. "When we first met, Mark was just another American…how do you say…renegade. He was very angry. Very bitter. But he had passion, and in time, he had love. And I had love for him too."

She brushed Dexter's arm. "I have something that belongs to him. And I need to know what happened to him. It is very important to me. I cannot tell you how much."

Dexter turned the car on again. "Alright. You can come. But I have to warn you, there is something going on. It could be dangerous." He pulled out onto the road and started driving.

Caterina looked out the window and thought, *you have no idea.*

Chapter 15

Beverly smiled as she pulled her gray suit out of the closet. Stan would think it was because he asked her to wear it, and that was fine with her. The truth was, however, it was her best, "I-am-in-control" outfit. She wore it whenever she had a really important meeting. And this meeting in Detroit was important.

Unable to sleep, she had pulled the report Stan had given her out. The numbers and projections were detailed and complicated enough to push thoughts of Mark away, at least for a little while.

According to the report, Tierrasante had purchased long term leases on tracts of land all over the country over two decades before, paying a premium rate. Those high rates had guaranteed fixed minimum increases in state and local taxes for services. In effect, when those tracts of land were just sand dunes and swamplands, the government had been more than happy to collect taxes on services that weren't delivered.

Because of their inability or unwillingness to look at Tierrasante's long range plans, they were now in a situation where they could not, by law, significantly raise taxes on those properties without suffering a substantial fiscal penalty. Tierrasante was now able to develop those properties into affluent neighborhoods at a significant profit and the autonomy of each of those communities was guaranteed.

And developing them, they were. Already, five communities had been built, and two had just broken ground. Columbia Village, just outside of Philadelphia, was scheduled to break ground in a few months, and they had reached capacity over a year ago. The communities attracted many of the more influential citizens in each of the targeted areas, and that too, ensured the Villages' continued prosperity. With another twelve new communities scheduled to go up in the next five years, Beverly knew a great opportunity when she saw one. She was getting on board.

Her thoughts shifted again to Mark and the wedding that would not be. Maybe she had lost there, maybe not. But she was certainly going to win professionally. She was hurt, but she knew that eventually she'd get past it. In the meanwhile, she would throw herself into this project and secure a bright professional future. At least *that* she could do.

She was meeting Stan and the Reisling's at the Columbia site at ten. She and Stan had a one o'clock flight to Detroit. She had time for one more cup of coffee and then she'd get ready to meet her future.

• • •

While Beverly was pouring another cup of coffee, Stan was meeting with Greg Young. When Stan stepped out of his building to take his morning run, a limousine pulled up beside him. The dark glass rolled down and Young leaned out. "Get in."

When Stan got in, the window went up and the car started moving. Young ignored Stan while he poured a cup of tea. He took a sip and then turned to Stan. "Care for a cup? This is a wonderful blend I have imported from China."

Stan shook his head, "No…no thank you."

Young took another sip from his cup. "As you wish. I understand you are going out to Columbia Village today. Why wasn't I informed?"

Stan wiped his brow and turned to him. "I...uh...these people are on the approved list and are friends of Beverly's. I thought it might make the pot sweeter for her to join us if I pushed through with their approval before we go to Detroit."

Young nodded his head silently. "You thought....very well. I looked into Beverly's background. There is enough there to make her an asset to us, and sufficient ties to keep her with us. You, however, Mr. Towers, are beginning to be of some concern. There is no room for mavericks here. I make all decisions and those who work for me, do as I tell them. You don't seem to be able to grasp that concept.

"This project is too important to have anyone place it in jeopardy, Mr. Towers. I will remove anyone or anything that becomes an obstacle in my path. Do I make myself perfectly clear?"

Stan swallowed hard as he nodded.

Young picked up his tea and took another sip. "Good. Because we won't have another conversation about this—that is, if this issue comes up again, I will use another form of persuasion, which I am certain you will find *very* unpleasant."

Young put his cup down and dabbed his mouth with the linen napkin. "Well then, as long as we are clear, on to other business. I have another project for you. We are having some...unforeseen difficulties in Detroit, which will require us to move more quickly on that project. There are a few parties that need to be brought into the community immediately. You and your associate will meet with them tomorrow morning, and you will sign them. Do I make myself clear? The profiles will be provided to you when you check into your hotel."

Stan tried to maintain his composure, turning to look Young in the eye. "Of course, no problem Mr. Young. I will have to contact Beverly immediately and let her know of the change in plans. We were scheduled to fly in and out tonight."

Young tapped on the glass panel, and immediately the car pulled over and stopped. "Then I suggest you do that, Mr. Towers." He opened the door. Stan was surprised to find that they were parked in front of his building. They must have been circling his block the entire time.

As Stan stepped out of the car, Young leaned forward and said, "I will see you in Detroit, Mr. Towers. I'd like to have dinner with your beautiful associate. Make the necessary arrangements."

Young started to roll the window up and had another thought. As it stopped half way down again, Stan could see Young's eyes shining at him as he added, "Oh, and Stan? I enjoyed our little ride, but I am not really a morning person. I suggest you not do anything that will make me get up so early again." The window went back up and Young disappeared. Stan watched as the car wound it's way down the block and out of sight.

He sat heavily on his stoop, wondering if his pounding heart would explode. *What had he gotten himself into? What was he getting Beverly involved in?*

Stan went into the bathroom and splashed cold water on his face. Grabbing a towel, he looked into the mirror and thought, *Stan, my man, you've have gotten yourself into a mess.* Stan had no illusions about Young's threat. He would kill him if he had to and Stan had no intention of letting that happen. There was a lot of money to be made and Stan was going to have a piece of it.

Stan knew what he had to do. No blue-collar, illiterate peasant in an expensive suit was going to get the best of Stan Towers. Squaring his shoulders determinedly, Stan walked confidently to the phone and dialed Beverly's number. It rang three times before Beverly picked up.

"Hello?"

"Beverly, it's Stan, I'm glad I caught you. Listen, I'm running, so I'll have to make this fast. Our trip to Detroit is going to be a bit longer than we anticipated. You should plan to be there for two days, three tops, so pack accordingly. Things are speeding up out there and we are going to be at the right place at the right time."

"Three days, Stan? I can't do that. I have deals pending and…a personal matter I have to attend to. I just can't be gone for three days right now."

"Bev, this is big. Garrison will have someone cover for you at the office. As for your personal life, I can't help you with that. I can help you with your professional future and that means you need to be there, Bev." He paused, "Bev, I need you there with me on this, okay?"

Beverly sighed heavily. "Fine, Stan, we'll talk about it later. I'll see you at Columbia shortly."

"You might have to start without me, Bev. I have to get over to the office first and pick up some papers, talk to Garrison. Why don't you start the tour with your friends and I'll join you as soon as I can."

They hung up and Stan headed for the shower. What he needed to do wouldn't take long. He smiled smugly as he stepped under the hot, streaming water. If Young wanted to play hard ball, so be it. Stan was a winner and he intended to win this one too.

• • •

Beverly hung up the phone and sat on the edge of the bed. Three days in Detroit when everything in her personal life was falling apart. What if Dexter called with information? What if Mark showed up and she wasn't here? She shook herself and stood.

This deal was important to her. Finding out about Mark was important too, but she couldn't just sit around waiting. It would drive her crazy and it wasn't productive. She would call Dexter and let him know where she'd be if he got any information, and Mark? Well, if Mark showed up after all this time, he'd have to understand and be patient until she returned, just like she'd been.

She dialed Dexter's number and when the machine clicked on, she left a message. She looked at the clock. It was already 9:15 A.M. Lauri would have already left for work and she had to get out to Columbia Village to meet the Reislings. She jotted a short note to Lauri, asking her to call her office and get her hotel information, secretly hoping that Lauri would have the opportunity to pass the information to Mark, and then quickly threw some things into a bag for the trip.

It was 9:30 A.M. when she tossed the bag into the trunk of her car, climbed in and pulled out of the garage. She'd have to speed to get out to the site on time. She prayed that the rush hour traffic had cleared as she gunned her engine and raced down the street.

• • •

The Reislings' black Mercedes 450 was parked in the driveway of the model home when Beverly drove up. As she cut the engine and climbed from the car, the Reislings got out of theirs and slammed the doors behind them. Doris Reisling, a petite woman in her early fifties, with professionally colored and quaffed auburn hair, smiled widely as she approached Beverly with open arms.

She was dressed in a brown tweed pants suit and soft leather loafers. Her skin was tanned and smooth, the results of having a tanning bed in their home workout room, and a good friend who happened to be the most sought after plastic surgeon in the city. As she hugged Beverly warmly, Beverly took in Doris' expensive perfume and thought to herself again, that money made all the difference in how one handled the aging process.

"Beverly, how wonderful it is to see you again. It's been ages. You look wonderful."

Beverly returned the embrace. "Doris, you are looking fabulous. Did you just get back from a vacation?"

Doris laughed, "Heaven's no. Who has time for vacations? I just make sure I don't miss my weekly beauty sessions. How is that man of yours? Ronald?"

Beverly decided not to correct her. What was the point? Doris had known all of them since their university days and had not once, called Mark by his name. "He's fine, Doris. Out of town as usual."

Doris took her arm and they strolled over to her husband, who stood by the car watching them and smiling. She leaned over to Beverly and whispered, "Well, enjoy it while you can, dear. When he is home every night, with dirty socks on your sofa watching football and spilling crumbs into the rug, you'll miss these days."

"I'm looking forward, Doris. Looking forward."

"Looking forward to what?" Michael Reisling gave Beverly a brief hug.

"Oh, nothing sweetheart, just girl talk."

Michael grunted, "Girl talk. Well, can we get in to see this model? You girls can talk later. I have an 11:30 meeting I can't miss."

Beverly took his arm and kissed his cheek. "Michael, you never change. It's good to see you."

Michael smiled a little, and then relaxed. "I'm sorry, Beverly. Doris has been talking of nothing else, since I told her you were working on these properties. Thank you for getting us this tour."

"Anything for old friends, Michael. I think you are going to enjoy this."

They walked up to the front door. Stood back and studied the exterior of the house as Beverly slipped the key into the lock.

"Are all of the homes a similar style?"

Doris walked back to him and looked up at the second floor windows. "I think it's lovely, Beverly." She turned to Michael and whispered, "Honey, at least give it a look, alright? For me?" She gave Michael a kiss and squeezed his hand.

Beverly turned from the door and answered, "No. That's one of the beauties of each Village. There are eleven styles of homes in each Village, but no house is the same as the next. Each home has a unique floor plan. Of course, they all use similar plumbing design and appliances, that sort of thing, but I think you'll find this house quite to your liking, Michael. Why don't we take a look inside."

She opened the door and stood aside as the Reislings entered.

As they looked around the spacious, sunny living room and made their way through the dining room and into the kitchen, Beverly continued.

"Columbia Village is the seventh community built by Canterbury, and there are several more around the country in the planning stages. In addition to owning your own home in a secure, exquisitely maintained and exclusive community, Canterbury offers its members very attractive benefits. For example, each village has at least one four-star hotel, and Canterbury residents can stay overnight at any of the sister hotels across the country at 50% off the advertised daily rates. Additionally, Canterbury offers its own financing, which entitles you to unsecured platinum memberships with all of the national major credit card companies. Canterbury residents also enjoy carte blanche memberships at 70 private recreational and social clubs nationwide."

Doris was strolling, rapturously through the kitchen, her manicured fingernails grazing the granite countertops lovingly.

"Nice, isn't it? Toshi Hontel, a world-renowned, award winning, Japanese interior designer, designed this kitchen. Don't you love the clean lines, light and creative use of space?"

Doris turned to Michael, her face dreamy, "Oh, dear, a fireplace in the kitchen." She turned to Beverly. "Would our house have something like this, Beverly?"

Beverly smiled, "This *is* your home, Doris. That is, if you decide to take it."

Doris turned back to her husband and put her arms around his neck and hugged him, "Oh Michael."

Michael Reisling gave Beverly a stern look over his wife's head. He disengaged from her embrace, turning his frown to an indulging smile as he said, "Honey, why don't we take a look at the upstairs before we start packing our things." He turned to Beverly, "Which way?"

Beverly started to lead the way to the staircase, when Michael stopped her. "Can we go up alone? We need to have a few minutes of privacy."

Beverly looked at Doris. She could tell that as far as Doris was concerned, there was only a question of where they'd put their furniture and what kind of window dressings they'd choose for the huge bay windows in the living room. She smiled.

"Of course, Michael. The stairs are just on the other side of the dining room. There are three bedrooms and two baths upstairs. The master bedroom has a private bath, of course, and it is fitted with a 2-person jacuzzi and a sauna. I'll be in the living room if you need me." She stepped aside so the Reislings could go upstairs. Doris squeezed her arm as she passed Beverly and winked. The house was sold.

Chapter 16

Dexter and Caterina drove in silence, down the dark, winding roads. As they passed over a hill, Dexter could see lights in the distance and Caterina pointed ahead, saying "that is it."

As they neared the shantytown, the silence was broken by music and other sounds of life. The deserted roads gave way to a bustling little city and Dexter had to slow his car almost to a crawl, as beautiful children, barefoot and ragged, ran through the streets. Women talked and laughed from windowsills, dogs barked, someone was singing a drunken song somewhere in the shadows. Men sat in straw chairs on tumbling porches, smoking cigars, drinking beer, playing cards.

"Park here." Caterina commanded.

Dexter pulled over, hearing a broken bottle crunch under the tires. Caterina jumped out of the Jeep as Dexter locked the car doors. She walked over to an old man sitting on the steps of a store.

"Senhor, where can I find the Manteloga home?"

The old man looked past Caterina to Dexter, assessing his watch and ring. Caterina chastised him in rapid Portuguese and the man lowered his

eyes and pointed down the alleyway. As they walked away, Dexter took his
watch and ring off and stuffed them in his pocket.

They picked their way through the debris and came out on a dimly lit
street. They stood on the steps of the first house, deciding whether or not
to knock, when three young boys rushed them from behind, knocking
Caterina to the ground and pushing Dexter up against the wall. One boy
grabbed for Dexter's wallet, but was not fast enough. Dexter grabbed his
arm and spun him against the wall, using his other forearm to knock the
second boy to the ground. The third boy pulled out a knife and prepared
to lunge at Dexter, but Caterina rolled towards him, clipping him behind
the knee and bringing him to the ground with a thud. A second later,
Caterina had the knife in her hand and at the boy's throat.

Dexter grabbed the other two boys by the scruff of their necks and
threw them down beside the third. "What should we do with them?"

Caterina's face was grim. She answered him in Portuguese, "We should
cut their thieving throats." When the boys howled in horror, Caterina
turned her head slightly towards Dexter and winked. She turned back to
the cowering boys and slapped each of them before she let them up. They
ran into the darkness followed by a hail of Caterina's curses.

When they were gone, Caterina turned to Dexter. He was smiling
appreciatively and nodding his head. "You are something else, Caterina.
You've got some moves."

"It's called *capoeira*, an Afro-Brazilian form of martial arts."

"You weren't bad either, a little slow, but then again, you're a suburban boy."

Dexter and Caterina jumped and turned to the voice. Caterina let out
a small yelp and crossed herself. "Santa Maria de..."

Mark came out from the shadows, grinning widely. He was limping,
leaning on a stick. His face was battered and bruised, his clothes torn and
bloody. He smiled first at Caterina, then turned to Dexter. "Hey man,
nice to see you."

Dexter sputtered, "Nice to—aw man!" He hugged Mark, then let him go. "You never cease to amaze me, Ace. You look like crap. But better than a dead man."

Caterina walked slowly over to Mark and touched his face gently. "Thank God you are alive. Ah Mark." She went into his arms.

Mark stroked her hair and looked over her head at Dexter, whose mouth was turned down in a frown as he understood the intimacy of their moment. He thought about Beverly's face when he'd told her about Mark.

Caterina stepped back to study Mark and wiped her tears. Then cursing him, she slapped his face and stalked back to the Jeep. Mark smiled as he watched her leave.

"So, what the hell is going on, Mark? What happened to you? Everyone thinks you're dead—a crash in some mountains running drugs."

"Yeah right. Man, you know me better than that."

Dexter looked at Mark hard. "I thought I did, but then, the Mark I thought I knew wouldn't have disappeared into Brazil without a word," he paused, "not even to his fiancée or best friend."

Mark looked off and said, "Well, that is true. The Mark you knew wouldn't have, huh? A lot of things have changed, Dex. We can talk about that later. I was not running drugs, but I did crash. That crash was an ambush."

"You mind, man? My leg's still bothering me." They walked over to a low wall and leaned against it. Mark continued.

"There were three, maybe four in on it, I couldn't identify them if they were standing here in front of me. Must've used a Stinger. The druggies have an arsenal of high tech arms, thanks to the black market. Anyway, I was flying this sister into Salvador and the helo caught fire. Man, they were waiting for us in the brush. They came at us with automatics. I tried to take off again, but they pulled the woman out of the helo. I tried to go back for her, man. But the control panel went up in flames.

"I tried to pull up, but couldn't get over the tree line and went down hard. I jumped, hit the trees and was knocked out cold. The copter blew up. I don't know what they did with the woman. She's probably dead. She was a sister too."

Mark grabbed the front of Dexter's shirt. "I got a plan though, and you gotta help me find those heads."

Dexter backed away from the wall, holding up his hands. "Hold on, Mark. This isn't Philly. We're in their backyard."

"We can take em out, Dex. Just like old times...remember Zuwarah?"

"Hey, hey! You don't even know who they are. How are we supposed to track them? And even if we do find them, then what? Do we strap on a couple of M-60s and go up against an army? Right."

"Listen to you. Those punks tried to blow my brains out, they kidnapped and probably killed a sister and you're saying, what—forget it? You're not going to back me on this, bro? Fine. Go back home to your safe desk job and I'll take care of this myself. I should have known I couldn't count on you. This is a man's job," Mark sneered.

"Playing out suicide fantasy missions does not make you a man, Mark."

"Why are you down here anyway, G-man? Come to read me the Constitution?"

"Your mother asked me to come down and pick up your effects."

Mark tossed him his wallet. "Yeah? Well take that and go on back home. Tell them all you found were ashes, man. They'll have a memorial service, you'll be a hero, hell, Beverly might give even you some play. Yeah, maybe you might be able to finally get her with me out of the way."

Mark watched Dexter's stricken face and pressed the knife in further. "That's right. I know you still want her. But she wanted a man. Not a G-suit with a badge."

Dexter punched Mark in the jaw, knocking him to the ground. Mark just laughed as he got up, rubbing his jaw. "Did I touch a raw nerve?"

Dexter took a step towards Mark, but Mark put up a hand. "Come on, Dex, don't front me. You know you've been sweating Bev ever since we got together. Who did you think you were fooling?"

Dexter swallowed hard and looked off into the night. "G-suit with a badge. That's very good, Mark. Tell me something bro—when are you going to grow up?"

Dexter took a few steps closer to Mark, looking him hard in the eye. "Have you ever considered that there are people back home that might need you?" Dexter shook his head.

"Probably not. You've been too busy blaming 'The Man' and running away from reality. Look at you—Homey the Clown with a passport. It was funny in school, but we aren't undergrads anymore, Mark, and this isn't funny. You have a woman who loves you and yeah, I loved her too, but she chose you Mark,—Not me. Fine. I've had to live with that. But the minute your life gets hard, you just say 'fuck it' and everyone who cares about you and run off? Maybe we are all better off thinking you're dead.

"And as far as Beverly is concerned, that was my bust for thinking you knew how to treat a true lady. I thought you could do better than this, but I guess not."

Mark just smiled. "You haven't changed. I see you are still the pompous, self-righteous tight ass you always were."

Dexter shoved his hands in his pocket and shook his head. "Yeah? Well, maybe so. But this rerun you're playing in isn't working for you. This time someone tried to cast you as a permanent dead man. And if you don't find a new role, you'll get a call back sooner than you think."

Dexter headed towards the alley, then turned back. "I'll tell them I couldn't find you. But you'd better watch your back, Ace. If someone went to this much trouble to take you out, they won't give up that easily. And you, my man, are running out of places to hide. Good luck." He turned and walked away, disappearing into the alleyway.

Chapter 17

Dexter stalked back to the car, clenching and unclenching his fists. He knew his anger was not just about Mark having walked away from his life—and Beverly. Part of his anger was at himself.

Dexter had always been cautious and had played by the rules. He had been told he'd get the brass ring if he studied hard and got good grades; didn't drink too much, respected people and his elders. If he found a career that gave him a solid future and stayed with it until he retired with a lofty title and gold-plated watch, he'd have the respect of the world. Well, Dexter was well on his way. A successful Naval Intelligence officer and now a senior analyst with the U.S. Secret Service. He had done it all, while Mark, who had always made his own rules and the devil be damned, who'd said what he thought and did as he pleased, had won the true prize.

Beverly had walked out of Dexter's safe and secure life and into Mark's irresponsible, self-absorbed arms. And good old, steady Dexter had stood by and watched like a gentleman, settling for friendship while his heart was being ripped from his chest.

He'd stood by and watched while they fell in love, made plans to marry, have a home and family, everything Dexter had dreamed of and worked for—and Mark had gotten. And now Mark was throwing it all away in a moment of self-pity. If that had not been enough to make Dexter want to kill him, Mark had laughed in Dexter's face while he did it.

Mark had wounded Dexter with his carefully aimed dart. Dexter hadn't realized, until that moment, that he might still want Beverly back; that perhaps, unconsciously, he had hoped Beverly would change her mind. Maybe she'd wake up one morning and realize that she'd had enough of the uncertainty, the recklessness. Maybe Dexter had rushed to Philadelphia because he had allowed himself to hope that there might still be a chance. He didn't like to think of himself as a sideliner, but he realized that that was what he had become.

If he went back and told Beverly that she'd lost Mark in some heroic tragedy, Dexter would have to give up any hope of ever winning back her love. Forever after, he would be only a painful reminder of the man Beverly had loved and lost.

The hell with Mark, Dexter thought. He had told Beverly he loved her, proposed marriage to her, lied to her and everyone else—and then run off weeks before his wedding without a word. Mark didn't deserve his protection. He'd go back to the States and tell Beverly the truth. He leaned against his Jeep and sighed.

What really bugged him was that Mark had seen through him and probably always had. Dexter was the fool, and he didn't like knowing that at all. He gave the tire a frustrated kick, and then walked over to the car door and fished for his keys. Caterina unlocked the door, startling Dexter out of his reverie.

"Caterina. I didn't expect you to still be here. Why did you wait?"

Caterina looked straight out through the windshield and answered tightly, "I can't drive."

Dexter climbed in and pulled off. He drove for a while without comment, then turned to Caterina. "That must have been quite a shock, seeing Mark alive."

Caterina answered thoughtfully, "Yes, it was."

The car was silent again for a little while, but Dexter didn't want to dwell on his dark thoughts. He forced himself to grin slightly, as he turned to Caterina. "That was some pretty fancy footwork back there."

Caterina smiled slightly. "Yes, well I am a woman of…hidden talents." She paused and then looked out the window and asked, "is Mark returning to the States with you?"

Dexter pressed his lips together tightly and handed Caterina the wallet Mark had given him. "No. He'll be staying on here."

Caterina kept her face turned so Dexter would not see the tears of relief welling in her eyes. "Ahh," was all she said. They drove off in silence.

• • •

"Let me out here. I want to walk the rest of the way." Caterina pulled out a key and handed it to Dexter. "This is the key to Mark's place. You can stay there tonight."

Dexter pulled over into the grass by the side of the dark, deserted road. The lights of Ilhéus twinkled dimly in the distance.

Dexter caught Caterina's arm as she climbed out of the car, then smiled and loosened his grip to a gentle touch. "I was going to tell you it was too dangerous out there…but we both know now that you can take care of yourself. So I'll just ask if you'll be alright."

Caterina looked as if she were struggling with a decision. Then she took a breath and said, "I just found out that the man I love—who I was mourning as dead—is alive. I need to think about that. What that means to me—and to him. I also have some business I need to attend to." She withdrew her arm, squeezing Dexter's hand as she stepped away from the car. "I will see you in the morning."

• • •

Caterina stood on the side of the road and watched Dexter's car disappear around the bend. Then, she turned and picked her way down a narrow path leading into the trees. On the other side of the copse there was a cottage. She sat down on a rock, careful not to be seen from the lighted window. Her eyes filled with angry tears.

Mark was alive. For two days, she had been tearing her hair out from guilt and remorse. Chang's poison was seeping into every corner of her life.

Was it not enough, she wondered, that she had spent years planning her escape from the hell of her life in Cuba, a forced co-conspirator of Castro's reign of terror, only to find herself a spy and a mistress for Edward Chang's dirty world of drugs and domination?

Edward had been a minor player for Tierrasante back then. He had been stationed in Cuba for a few months and had charmed his way into Caterina's confidence and bed. When she shared with him her dream of escaping, he had helped her flee Cuba with her father and over $50,000 of Castro's blood money. He gave them the papers necessary to start again in Brazil under an assumed name. Then, he'd turned it against her. He threatened exposure and extradition to gain her silence, and then threatened death to the family she'd left behind in Cuba to ensure her loyalty.

It was Edward who had ordered her to the bed of the newly arrived American. The organization wanted information about anyone who came into their little base town, and this American, Mark, had come without bags or tourist books. They wanted to know why. When it was discovered that Mark was an ex-pilot for the U.S. armed forces, they'd wanted to bring Mark into "the family." Mark had rebuffed those initial advances, and so Caterina had been sent in to try another form of persuasion.

At first, it hadn't mattered to Caterina. After all, he was just some American, hiding out. She couldn't afford to care about him—when her family's safety was at stake. She'd seduced him and insinuated herself into his life. But she found that Mark was a good man. He was running from something, she knew that, but it wasn't something illegal. He was a man of principle and honor and had treated her with kindness and respect.

And she'd fallen in love with him.

She didn't know, at first, that he was the pilot who'd taken Toni into the mountains for the drop off of the latest cache of newly laundered drug money. It was only after she'd been summoned to this cottage the day before, that she'd been told of the botched mission. She'd been ordered to find evidence of Mark's death in that crash, or find him and eliminate him—there could be no witnesses—and report back when the job was done.

It had been all she could do, not to reveal her horror that Mark might be dead. She'd walked away from the cottage hoping she would merely have to mourn the loss of the first man she'd ever loved, rather than find him and kill him. When he'd stepped out of the shadows, there in the favela, she had almost died with relief. She hadn't lost him. He was alive, and now they were all in terrible danger, unless she could think of some way to save them all.

It was getting late. She stood, shaking the leaves and dirt from her skirt and brushed the wallet Dexter had given her. She pulled it out and stared at it, making a decision. She could at least buy them some time. She walked up to the door, knocking a code.

A moment later, the door opened by a man wearing a shoulder holster. She stepped inside and allowed herself to be frisked by a second man. A third man, similarly armed, stood guard at the one, front facing window. She looked past him to the sofa.

Toni turned and motioned to Caterina. "Sit down. You're late."

Caterina remained where she stood. "I was held up."

Toni's eyes narrowed, "Did you find out anything about that pilot?"

Caterina looked Toni hard in the eye, and tossed her Mark's wallet as she answered, "Yes. Mark Davis is dead."

Chapter 18

Stan pulled in behind Beverly's car and turned off the motor. "Yes, things are going great. I'll have enough to buy a Level I by May…about one point two mil…that's right. Hey, Providence certainly doesn't need my money. Canterbury provides its own financing…Let's just say…"

Stan saw the front door of the house open. Beverly stepped out on the porch and waved at him. "Gotta go. Call you tonight." He disconnected the call and put the phone in his inside jacket pocket.

Beverly walked down the pathway to meet him. "So? How's it going in there?"

She took Stan's arm and leaned her head towards him, speaking softly, "I think it's a done deal. They're up on the second floor now, looking over the space, talking.

"I'll tell you though, I thought Doris was going to die when she walked in. She was flipping through her organizer for names of moving companies before they made it to the second floor!"

Stan squeezed her hands. "Congratulations. I told you this would be a breeze."

"Well, this place really sells itself. I'll tell you, Stan, I'd probably be foaming at the mouth myself if could afford a place like this."

Stan laughed. "Darlin', this house is peanuts compared to what you'll be able to buy after a few months on the team." They climbed the steps and entered the foyer.

Stan whispered, "Especially if you keep doing what you're doing now." He nodded toward the stairs, where Doris and Michael had just appeared.

Beverly disengaged from Stan and walked over to the Reislings. "Stan, I'd like you to meet Dr. Michael Reisling and his wife, Doris. Folks, this is my associate, Stan Towers, the man who has made this possible."

Stan gave Michael a hearty hand pump. "Good to meet you, Dr. Reisling." He turned to Doris and extended his hand. "And Mrs. Reisling, how do you like your new home?"

Michael cut in before Doris could answer. "Not so fast, Mr. Towers. This isn't "our" home until we've discussed a few important details."

Stan recovered quickly. "Of course, of course. Well folks, why don't we have a seat in the living room and have a chat. I'm sure I can answer any questions you might have." He stepped aside so they could pass. Then he turned to Beverly, "After you?"

Beverly whispered back, "Don't worry about Michael. He's always gruff. He's a tough customer, but he always gives Doris what she wants—and she wants this house."

Beverly's cell phone rang. As she pulled it out, she said to Stan, "Why don't you get started. I'll take this call and join you in a sec."

Stan gave Beverly the thumbs up and went in to join the Reislings. Beverly turned on the phone. "Beverly," she answered.

It was Robin, the office receptionist. "I'm sorry to disturb you Ms. Madsen, but I have a Dexter Racine on the line, insisting that I track you down."

Beverly's heart caught, "Thank you. Put him through…Dex?"

The line crackled. "Hey, Bev…I'm in…Brazil…I…"

Beverly shouted into the phone, "Hello? Hello, Dexter? I can't hear you…Brazil?…What are you doing…wait…hold on, I'm going to go outside, maybe the connection will be clearer."

She stepped out on to the porch. "Dex, are you still there? Did you say you were in Brazil?"

"Yes…I found…and Mark…"

Beverly tried another channel, but the call didn't get any clearer. "Dex, did you say you found Mark? Dex, can you hear me?"

"We talked and…but I can go more into…I get back to the States…I have…tomorrow. I'll call you when…"

"Did you say that Mark was in Brazil?"

"Yes…when I…so then it…but we can…tomorrow night."

"Dexter I can't make out what you're saying. Can you call back? Or give me your number? Dex? Dex??!" The call had disconnected. Beverly wanted to scream with frustration. She redialed the office number.

"Robin, this is Beverly. Did you get a number on that last call?"

"Why, no Ms. Madsen, was I supposed to?"

Beverly's shoulders slumped. "No, you didn't know. Listen, if Mr. Racine calls again, get a number, it's extremely important. I'm heading for Detroit this afternoon, so if he calls back, get his number and give him my contact number in Detroit."

"Will do, Ms. Madsen."

"I'll check in when I get to the hotel. Thanks Robin." Beverly disconnected and tossed the phone it in her bag.

The front door opened and Stan and the Reislings stepped out on the porch. Beverly struggled to push back the threatening tears. Regaining composure, she turned to them with a smile. Stan and Doris were beaming. Michael Reisling had a look of long suffering defeat. She turned back to Doris. "So? How goes it?"

Stan cut in, "Beverly, may I have the honor of introducing to you the newest members of Columbia Village?"

Doris couldn't contain herself. She burst from the porch and gave Beverly a choking hug. "I can't thank you enough for what you've done. I simply can't wait to get through all the paperwork so we can move in."

Michael's stern countenance melted as he watched his wife. He grinned a little when he caught Beverly watching him. "Looks like you've got us, Bev. Thanks, really, for making this happen. Doris will be—I mean *we* will be very happy here."

Beverly smiled back. "I know you will be, Michael. I know you will."

Chapter 19

"This is an Eyewitness News election week update. With the hotly contested, democratic gubernatorial primary days away, former Lieutenant Governor Richard Chase' office announced that the governor has approved the construction of Mount Clemens Village. The governor's go ahead on this project, publicly supported by Richard Chase, is estimated to bring 2,000 new jobs and more than twelve million dollars in revenue to the Detroit area. This approval, given so close to the primary, is certain to secure Chase' victory in the primaries."

Chang turned the volume down on the television set and pushed the button on his intercom. "Get Toni on the line for me immediately."

Getting up from the armchair, Chang paced the floor of his suite. Things were going better than expected. There had been no more newscasts on the money laundering allegations and his sources in Washington had informed him that, although there had been some talk of an investigation, no one had been sent out to Detroit to investigate Chase' campaign books. Thanks to Tierrasante's funds, Chase was in position to win the primaries, which assured his place in the governor's mansion, with Edward Chang standing behind him, pulling his puppet's strings.

All that remained unfinished here, was the meeting scheduled later in the evening, where the last few people who could potentially interfere with his plans would be reeled into the Tierrasante web, and Toni's report that her mess in Brazil had been successfully cleaned up. His private, secured line phone rang. It was Toni.

"We've received proof that the pilot was killed in the crash, Edward. I'm booked on a flight back to Detroit tomorrow morning. How is it going up there?"

"Everything is moving smoothly and according to plan. We meet with the investors later this evening and approval on Mount Clemens was just announced on national television. We'll meet with Chase as soon as you get in. Our boy has just secured the nomination."

"Wonderful. Listen, Ed, your little friend has completed her work here. Do you have anything more for her?"

Chang thought about the lovely little Cuban temptress. How nice it would have been to have gotten down there once more to see her. He shrugged. Ah, well, such was life.

"No. Her contract has been filled. We can release her from service. But why don't you have Larry...talk to her after you've gotten back here? Can't afford to have you held up there any longer. Oh, and make certain she has no further concerns on the Cuban issue as well."

"Understood. Consider it done." Toni paused, her voice dropping to a more intimate tone. "I can't wait until this election is over, Ed. I miss being with you."

"We are almost done here, love. Just keep being wonderful. We'll have a car waiting for you at the airport. I'll see you tomorrow."

Chang hung up the phone. With Caterina removed permanently from Ilhéus, he would have to move his Brazilian operation to another city. Perhaps this time, he'd simply station Toni there. Temporary operatives were too much trouble. Still, he considered, Caterina had been an amusing diversion. She was smart and a skilled soldier. It was too bad her loyalty was only his by force. He could have used a woman like that here in the States.

He picked up an envelope and emptied its contents. A picture of Beverly was on top of the pile. He picked it up and studied the face smiling at him. She could be that operative here and he was looking forward to working with her. Once she was in the family, there would be no further use for Stan Towers. He'd have no regrets removing Stan. Had Beverly signed on with Greg at lunch that day, Stan would never have returned from their early morning ride.

He'd been ordered by Young to arrange the eventual elimination of the troublesome Stan Towers, but to do so more carefully than he had taken care of Caterina. Unlike Caterina, who was a fugitive living in Brazil with false papers, Stan was the son of a U.S. Senator. Once Caterina's family in Cuba was disposed of, there would be no one ever looking for her. That would not be the case with Stan. A sloppy job would mean an investigation, and the Senator had the influence and connections to institute a thorough manhunt.

Chang dropped Beverly's picture on the pile of papers and went to the bar. He poured a drink and took a thoughtful sip. He had time to work that problem out. In the meanwhile, the details of the investors' meeting and dinner with Beverly had to be taken care of.

• • •

Dexter handed his passport over to the official and checked his watch. Two hours and he would be boarding a plane for Miami. He had decided to go directly to Philadelphia to talk to Beverly before heading home. He hadn't thought it a good idea to tell her about Mark over the phone, especially since she had sounded so upset when he'd called earlier.

The official handed Dexter his papers and tipped his hat, smiling politely. Dexter figured he had time for a cup of coffee, maybe call in to the office to see what was going on and to let Bremmer know he'd be back sooner than he had expected.

He thought about Mark again, leaning against that wall in the favela, telling Dexter to go back home and tell everyone he was dead. He recalled the way Mark's face had looked when he'd suggested Dexter might finally get Beverly—and the softer face he'd worn when he held Caterina. He thought about Caterina too. He'd stopped by the front desk earlier that morning to say good bye, but Caterina wasn't there. The old man pretended he didn't speak enough English to answer Dexter's questions about where he might find her. Resigned, he had finally written a brief note, thanking her for her help and saying goodbye, and headed out to the airport.

Dexter used his credit card to connect with his office. While he waited for his call to be transferred to Bremmer's office, Dexter scanned the airport lobby. He was surprised at how bustling it was, particularly because it was midweek and slow travel time for tourists. Instead of the usual display of expensive "play" clothes, chic linen suits and straw fedoras, designer beach ensembles and canvas espadrilles, most of the people moving around wore the plain clothes of the *fazenda* workers—those who labored on the wealthy plantations that dominated the region. Strident British voices, the staccato bursts of German dialogue, were absent from the low hum of excited travelers. There was only the musical ebb and flow of the locals.

Dexter was thinking how nice it might have been to have visited this beautiful place under other circumstances. He saw himself holding Beverly's hand as they strolled through Pelourinho in Salvador, laughing and talking as they sat at one of the center's outdoor cafe trying tasty *mariscada* seafood stew. His daydreams were interrupted by Bremmer's voice booming through the receiver.

"Dex—that you?"

"I'm here," he answered.

"I hope you've finished up your business, we could use you up here."

"Listen, I need to make a stop in Philly before I head up. Can you cover for me until tomorrow afternoon?"

"Sure, are you O.K.?"

Dexter remembered how distraught Beverly had sounded on the phone. His mind did a quick calculation and he knew he couldn't fly into Miami, get down to Philly and still be in Washington in the morning. Well, Beverly had waited this long, another couple of days before he broke her heart with Mark's news might be a blessing. He'd call her when he got into Detroit.

"Hey, Dex? You there?"

"Yeah, yeah. All right. I'll try to call when I get to Miami."

Dexter hung up the phone and stuffed his wallet back into his pocket. He turned. Standing behind him was Mark, dressed in local beggar's clothes and wearing sunglasses. "We have to talk." Mark turned and shuffled towards the entrance of the lobby. He turned briefly to see that Dexter was following him, and then went out on to the street.

Chapter 20

"Mr. Chase, you have a call on line one. It's Mr. Chang."

Chase looked up from a pile of papers and waved the aide away. "Tell him I'm not available and get a message. And close the door behind you. I don't want to be disturbed."

When the door closed, he threw down his pen and got up. This was going to be problem, shaking Chang loose. Chase was feeling pretty good about the polls. It was a done deal, his nomination from the party, his seat in the governor's office. His coffers were full. Chang's real estate deal was approved. Chase felt that he'd done his part, and now that his victory was assured, he didn't want Chang lurking around anymore.

He was aware that Chang thought he'd bought the next governor, but he was wrong. Chase had no intention of letting some half-breed hoodlum pull his strings. They'd both gotten what they'd bargained for, their business was concluded. Now, all he had to do was figure out how to get rid of him.

He picked up his internal line. "Charles, any word on when Toni is getting back?"

"Sir, she is flying into Miami, and then catching a connecting flight into Detroit. She's expected in tonight at 10:05 P.M."

"Fine. Have someone meet her at the airport. I need to meet with her *this* evening. I don't care how tired she is. Understand?"

"Yes sir, I'll get on it immediately."

Chase hung up the phone. Toni was the only person on his personal staff that was aware of the deal he'd made with Chang. She was therefore, the only one he could openly discuss the method of how to get rid of him. With the convention less than forty-eight hours away, he didn't have much time, and he didn't need the aggravation. He picked up the phone again.

"Sir?"

"On second thought, call the Miami airport and find out if you can arrange an immediate charter for Toni. I need her back here pronto. Then get a hold of her and make sure she gets on that plane. Let me know when it's arranged."

"Yes sir."

Chase hung up the phone again and went to the bar. Pouring a finger of scotch, he tossed it back quickly and slammed the glass down on the counter. He was going to be the next governor, damn it. And nothing, and no *one* was going to jeopardize that.

• • •

Toni reached over to the table beside the bed and hung up the phone. Edward's voice had reminded her that, while interludes with Larry were always entertaining, she was looking forward to returning to her man. She picked up an envelope sitting on the table beside the phone and handed it to Larry, who was laying beside her, smoking a cigarette.

"These are the instructions on how to contact me when you've completed the job." She smiled widely as she kissed him on the forehead and got up. "As always, it's been a pleasure working with you again, Larry."

She quickly showered, dressed and combed her hair. Coming out of the bathroom several minutes later, her makeup flawless, she stopped again at the bedside and ran her hand over Larry's hairy chest. "Hmmm. Pity we don't have more time."

Larry smiled back at her. "I'll get a shower and close the place up after you've gone. Have a safe trip home."

She left the bedroom and went to the front door of the cottage. The limousine was parked off to the side, the driver leaning lazily against the hood. She called him over. "Load my bags. We'll be leaving shortly."

Toni looked around the little cottage. It was really quite cozy. She always enjoyed her visits down to Ilhéus, although this trip had been more stressful than usual. She smiled as she remembered Mark's naïve observations about her. He'd told her she looked like a tourist, someone who didn't know of the dangers awaiting her in the wilds of Brazil. She chuckled. It was actually rather sweet, his gentlemanly efforts to save her when her men came at them that evening in the mountains.

He'd gotten her bag when he tried to pull her back into the helicopter. She hadn't told Edward that part. It didn't matter now anyway. The helicopter had crashed and exploded, destroying the bag and its contents, as well as the only witness to the drop site, which was less than a mile from their estate.

Had circumstances been different, she might have asked him to dinner, maybe enjoyed a night or two of his obvious talents. Certainly, she'd heard enough about him from Edward's little slut to have her interest piqued.

She thought about Caterina. Of course she knew that Edward had bedded her. He always did, when a pretty new woman worked with them. She told herself it didn't matter to her. It was a long time ago after all, and she'd certainly had enough of her own liaisons in her travels to know that it was simply one of the perks of the business.

Besides, she was Edward's woman. She was the one who was always there when the others had come and gone. She was the one Edward had chosen to help him build his empire, and she was the one who shared the wealth that was pouring in from their ventures. Still, it gave her some satisfaction to know that Caterina, with her dark, soulful eyes, wild black curls and sultry sensuality, was being disposed of.

Toni closed the door behind her and climbed into the limousine. As the car pulled off, she put her sunglasses on and leaned forward to pour a glass of wine. She didn't see a figure move swiftly to the back of the cottage, a stiletto held in a small, gloved hand.

Chapter 21

Stan was feeling pretty pleased with himself, as he recalled his and Beverly's meeting at Columbia Village. He was certain that Young would make Beverly a generous offer, even if he had raked Stan over the coals for bringing her in without permission. Because, despite their growing success, they still needed polished, savvy professionals on their team to help legitimize them, and Beverly had the goods.

Stan was rarely self-reflective, but he was always realistic. He knew he was a good, if uninspired middleman, at best. It was his father's name and position that had been his ticket in to Tierrasante, and he intended to milk it for every cent he could. But Beverly?

Beverly was the *real* thing. She didn't need smoke and mirrors. What you saw was what you got. A classic, brilliant and skilled businessperson. Tierrasante wanted that—hell they *needed* that, and Beverly was the one to deliver it.

Although he had never admitted it to anyone, Stan had always recognized and admired Beverly's talents. *It didn't hurt that she was beautiful too*, he mused. There had been a time when Stan had hoped that he and Beverly might do more than just work together. The combination of beauty, brains and style was irresistible. But Beverly had made it clear, with incredible sensitivity to his pride, that her heart belonged to someone else.

After Stan's ego had healed a bit, he was able to see that the way she'd handled that situation, had been with a head for both their budding friendship and their working relationship. He was able to work around his attraction for Beverly, even though the whole episode had left him wanting her even more.

Well, he figured as he stacked the papers into his briefcase and closed it with a satisfied snap, *he might not be the one with the key to her heart, but he sure was the one who was handing her the passport to the winner's circle.*

The phone rang. Stan smiled as he picked up the receiver. "Stan Towers."

"Greg Young, Stan."

Stan sat back in his chair. His voice was strained as he forced a smile into his voice. "Well, this is a surprise. I expected you'd be in Detroit by now."

There was a pause, and then Young spoke again. "I am. We are having some unforeseen difficulties here, which will require us to move more swiftly on this project than we anticipated. There are certain parties here that will have to be brought into the community immediately. You will be meeting with them this evening and you will sign them on. Their profiles will be provided to you when you check into the hotel."

Stan tried to swallow down the lump in his throat before he continued. "Yes, of course. And Mr. Young, thank you for your confidence in me."

Young laughed. "It isn't confidence, Mr. Tower. It's a test. Your success or failure in this matter will determine whether or not you have what we need in this organization. You have enjoyed some of the bounties of success, Mr. Towers. I don't believe I have to tell you the consequences of failure."

"Of course not, sir. Beverly and I will prepare a presentation that will—"

"Ms. Madsen will not be in on that meeting, as she will be dining with me and my Operations Manager on the Detroit project, Edward Chang. I believe I am going to have her working with him on this project once she joins us officially. And Mr. Towers? She is to know nothing of your meeting tonight. Do you understand?"

Stan understood a veiled threat when he heard one. "Very good. I will deliver the results, Mr. Young."

"Good. Because I am having doubts about your place with us, Mr. Towers. This meeting will go far to allay those doubts. I'll be watching you." Young disconnected.

Stan leaned back in his chair, his heart pounding in his chest. *Stan, my man, you've have gotten yourself into a mess.* Young had a gun aimed right at his head. Stan had no illusions about Young's threat. He would kill Stan if he had to. Well, Stan had no intention of letting that happen. He had worked too hard, waited too long, to go down like that. *Besides,* Stan thought, he was a practical man.

When Stan first thought he might be able to move to Tierrasante, he had done a little digging, wondered where a piece of white trash like Young had acquired all the capital he had for a project so grand in scale.

He had found out that at least some of the money was straight out of the drug fields of Columbia. While he recognized the information as dangerous and important, he hadn't been particularly bothered by it. After all, this country had been built dirty money. Most of the scions of society had blood money at the core of their now, lily white, green-blooded hearts.

His own great-grandfather had made it rich during Prohibition, much of the wealthy south had bought their wealth with the lives of slaves, and northern blue bloods got their spoils from exploited and desperate immigrants. That's the way the world worked. So why should he care on where the money came from now? The trick was, of course, to make certain that he was not the one being exploited. When it started raining money, he intended to get drenched.

But Stan also knew what he had to do to ensure his well being, and no cheap piece of trailer trash in a hand-tailored suit, was going to get the best of him, or threaten his life. Young had underestimated him, and Stan intended to take advantage of his blind side.

He stared at the photograph camouflaging his secret wall safe. Stan had made copies of the Colonnade disks as his insurance policy against

Tierrasante. They were dangerous people he was working with—but they weren't going to get the best of Stan Towers.

Stan stood and straightened his suit. Beverly would be waiting for him. With a last look at the framed picture, Stan left the office to meet Beverly.

Chapter 22

Dexter picked up his bag and followed Mark out into the street. The sun blazed hot on his neck and he had to shield his eyes for a moment to allow them to adjust to the light. He spotted Mark leaning indolently against the edge of the building, just another invisible beggar on the busy streets. He walked over to him.

"What do you need to talk to me about, Mark? I thought our business was concluded last night."

Mark continued studying the passersby as he answered quietly, "Look man, we've been friends a long time. I didn't want you to leave here like we left it. I want to give you something."

He dug into his pocket and pulled out a wallet, slipping it to Dexter. "I went back to the crash site after we talked and found the bag I grabbed from that woman I was talking about. I had it in my hand when I jumped clear, but I lost it in the fall. I was hell bent on going after those bastards, so I went back to find it, hoping I would have someplace to start. That's her wallet."

Dexter opened it and pulled out an international driver's license. "Patricia Hughes. Okay, so what do you want from me?"

"Take another look at it. It's a fake."

Dexter pulled it closer and studied it. "You're right. But it's top of the line."

"Yeah, well that's not all she had in that bag. Dex, she had manuals on the interiors of helicopters and tools.

"So she was a helicopter freak. I'd think you, of all people, would appreciate something like that."

"I don't think so, my man. She had portions of each book highlighted. The schematics for the internal wiring was red-inked. The tools are for hi-tech wiring. She was in on it. She sabotaged that copter."

Dexter frowned as he studied the picture of the woman. "Look, Mark, I don't know what you think I can learn from this. I don't even know why you'd expect me to help you. These papers suggest she works with. Clemens development in Detroit."

Mark looked at Dexter for the first time and answered solemnly, "Cuz no matter what, we're brothers Dex. You might not agree with the choices I'm making here, but you'll just have to take my word when I say I thought it was the best of a lot of bad choices."

"And Beverly?"

Mark turned his face away and remained silent.

Dexter stuffed the wallet into his pocket. "All right shipmate. I'll see what I can find out."

Mark took Dexter's hand and shook it. "Thanks, man. I knew I could count on you."

Dexter studied his friend's face, still bruised and cut from the crash. "Yeah, well, you take care of that leg. I'll let you know what I find."

Dexter turned and walked slowly back to the lobby entrance. Mark called out to him, "I'll talk to you in a couple of days." Dexter nodded his head wearily, but didn't turn around again.

Mark watched him disappear into the building and was about to cross the street when a limousine pulled up in front of him. The driver got out and pushed him aside, "Out of the way, you filthy beggar," he cursed.

Mark stepped back and started to go around, as the driver opened the passenger door and a feminine leg appeared. He stopped to see the well-formed leg's owner, and was startled as he recognized Toni's face. "Hey—hey you," he shouted.

The other front door of the car opened and a muscled bodyguard quickly stepped out, blocking Toni from a potential threat. Several people turned to look at the beggar shouting in the streets, including two policemen. Mark put his head down and coughed, trying to cover his outburst. He put his hands up to the two men and smiled vaguely towards the policemen, backing away from the car and disappearing behind the building.

Chapter 23

Beverly sat at her desk, twirling her pen and smiling to herself. Although she believed that Columbia Village—the entire Tierrasante project, in fact—was an incredible opportunity for those able to afford its gilt-gated opulence, she hadn't expected the reaction she'd gotten from the Reislings.

Stan had told her that the houses sold themselves, but...Beverly's mind reeled at the possibilities. When Stan went full on board with Tierrasante, his commission would go up to ten percent. Ten percent! She was certain that they would offer her a similar platform if she joined them.

She'd be able to take care of her parents in real style; pay off their mortgage...even buy them a boat—like the one on the front of the brochure her father had kept hidden in his top desk drawer for the last fifteen years. They'd be able to retire, and her mother could finally write her Great American Novel, as she'd always wanted.

And she and Mark's children would go to the best schools, they'd travel the world. Why when she told Mark—

Mark. Beverly's elation dimmed. Mark was missing—or perhaps he was simply gone. Beverly's mind flashed back to the brief phone call she'd gotten from Dexter. The line had been bad, Dexter's voice breaking up through the static, but she was certain she had heard Dexter say that Mark was in…Brazil?

Dexter had told her that Mark was out of the service, had been for months. But Beverly knew that they often reported that when Special Ops personnel were on secret missions. There could be no connections, no distractions…she'd seen just that sort of thing on made-for-TV movies. But this was real life and Dexter was in the service too. Surely they wouldn't have lied to him?

It was all so unbearable. If they had lied to Dexter to keep Mark's operation secret, Mark could be anywhere—hurt or even dead. If it were the truth—that Mark was not in the service anymore, then Mark had lied to her—probably all along. Everything—their wedding, his love, their life—was a sham.

Beverly wanted to scream. Why didn't Dexter call back? She reached for the phone and listened to the dial tone for a moment, before replacing the receiver. Who would she call? If there was an answer to be found, Dexter would find it. She'd have to trust that. Anxious, terrified, frustrated and angry by turns, Beverly wondered why Dexter hadn't called her back. Why hadn't Mark?

The phone rang, interrupting her thoughts. Taking a deep breath, Beverly sat up in her chair and picked up the receiver. "Beverly Madsen, may I help you?"

The phone crackled, "Beverly? Can you hear me?" It was Dexter.

"Oh my god, Dex?" Beverly gripped the phone. "Are you alright? Where are you? Did you say *Brazil*? Did you find Mark?"

"Hold it. Hold it! One question at a time. Are you sitting down?"

Beverly's heart was pounding in her chest. "Yes. What is it, Dex?"

"Well first, yes. I am in Brazil. And yes, I've found Mark."

"Brazil." Beverly sighed into the phone. In a stronger voice, she continued. "What are you—what is Mark doing in Brazil?"

The phone crackled, "Bev? Are you still there?"

"For heaven's sake, Dex! Yes, I'm still here—what are you and Mark doing in Brazil? Is he alright?"

"Yes, Bev. He was in a helicopter crash, but he's alive and kicking. A little bruised and battered, but he'll live." The static on the phone increased until Beverly could barely make out what Dexter was saying.

"…be flying back…and call you back from…okay?"

Beverly screamed into the phone. "Dex—I can't make out what you're saying. Are you and Mark coming home now? Dex? *Dex?!!*" The line went dead.

• • •

Toni dialed Edward's private line. When he picked up, she whispered, "Listen, my plane is boarding. We might have a problem. I think I saw that pilot a little while ago…yes, I know I told you he was dead. I thought so too. I had that Caterina look into it and she brought me back the man's wallet…I'm not even sure it was him, but I'm having some of the boys look into it. I just wanted to give you a heads up."

Toni paused, wondering whether or not she should tell Edward about the bag, just in case, and decided against it. She had seen Edward's rage. He was quick to destroy anything that even smelled like it might be a problem. She didn't want him sniffing around her. Particularly since she wasn't sure it really was Mark. Anyway, she reasoned, even if it were Mark, the bag would still have been destroyed, the crash had been real.

She wished, for a moment, that she had time to go back and take that lying little bitch, Caterina, out herself. Her only comfort was knowing she'd be dead before Toni reached Miami. The intercom announced last call for boarding.

"I have to go, Edward. I've taken care of it on this end, just don't want there to be any ugly surprises. If it was him, they'll find him. And this time, they have orders to bring me back his heart in a baggie. I'll see you tonight." Toni disconnected the call and picked up her bag.

Rushing to the gate, she handed the agent her ticket and went out to board. She was too preoccupied to notice the handsome black man climbing the stairs only four people in front of her.

Chapter 24

Bev hung up the phone and started pacing in the small space of her office. She looked at the report Stan had given her, sitting in the middle of the desk, and sat down again, wiping her tears. She didn't believe her life could possibly get more stressful. Mark was in Brazil, injured in a helicopter accident, she'd had two frustrating calls from Dexter, that left her more confused and scared than ever, and Stan handed her an exciting but potentially devastating bombshell opportunity. One that would force Emmanuel Garrison to close Canterbury down, and simultaneously make her rich.

She sat down at her desk again. She had to meet Stan in the lobby in just a few moments, so they could catch a cab together to the airport for the Tierrasante meetings in Detroit This trip that promised to yield a generous job offer and her first investors meeting on behalf of Tierrasante. She had to focus on that.

As for Mark, Dexter had said he was alright. She still didn't know if Mark was really on a mission, or had run out on her, but Dexter would have told her if anything had been seriously wrong. They were coming back, that much she had gotten from the brief phone call, though she didn't know when. There was nothing she could do until they got back to the States and called her. Reception had been advised to give them her contact number and schedule. That's all she could do.

That resolved as well as she could manage, Beverly forced herself to focus on Garrison and Canterbury. She knew Garrison would be devastated to learn he was losing two of his top people. She smiled to herself. He'd be devastated when he found his golden boy had jumped ship. Her leaving behind *that* news, would probably cause barely a ripple.

But, she acknowledged, *Emmanuel and Canterbury had been good to and for me*. She'd cut her teeth there, and found herself to be an accomplished negotiator and businesswoman. Garrison had always talked about looking out for number one—he'd just never considered that *she* might have been listening. He would weather the loss, she reasoned, and Tierrasante and Stan were leaving Canterbury with or without her.

If Tierrasante's business spelled the end of Canterbury Enterprises, there was nothing she could do to save them. Stan was right. She had an obligation to save herself. She had tried to convince Mr. Young to stay with Canterbury, which was the right and honorable thing to do. They had refused. She had worked hard to get where she was, and there was no point to her committing professional *hari kari*.

And the Colonnade project put people to work. Sure it was an exclusive community, but its doors weren't closed to minorities, the Reisling's were proof of that. In her new position, she could see to it that they were not the only ones.

The shrill ring of her telephone disrupted her reverie. Beverly looked at her watch and considered not answering it. It always happened that someone called as she was heading out the door with "just a quick question" that ended up being complicated and time consuming. She was to meet Stan in the lobby in about five minutes and had not even packed her briefcase or repaired her lipstick.

It rang a third time and Beverly sighed. She couldn't just let it ring. "Beverly Madsen," she answered in her most annoyed and hurried voice.

"Hey Bev, it's Dex. Am I coming in better now?"

Beverly sank back into her seat. "Yes. These calls are driving me crazy. Dexter, you said you were in Brazil? That you found Mark there too?"

There was a pause on the line, as Dexter considered what to tell her. Taking a deep breath, he said, "Yes. Mark is fine. The helicopter crash was pretty serious, but you know Mark—except for a couple of scrapes, he walked away. Anyway, I have to make this fast. Plans have changed a little. I'm heading for Detroit tomorrow when I leave here. Mark thinks the woman he was transporting sabotaged the craft, and Mark wants me to track her down in Detroit for him."

"What? Isn't he coming home too?"

"Look Bev, it's a long, complicated story and I can't go into it now. I think this is going to turn into a wild goose chase, but I promised Mark I'd look into it. I just wanted to let you know he's alright. I'll probably get down to Philly on Saturday and we'll talk at length. In the meanwhile, you take care of yourself and don't worry, okay? I'll be at the Hyatt, room 5671 tomorrow night, late if you need me. I gotta go, take care, okay?"

He hung up the phone. Beverly didn't know if the tears welling in her eyes were from anger or joy. Mark was alive, but not coming home. Dexter was in Brazil and heading for Detroit. 'Don't worry.' Dexter had told her. Was he kidding? She looked at her watch. Stan would be waiting for her in the lobby.

She picked up her briefcase. She couldn't, at this point, do anything about those men, but she could do something good for herself. Turning out the light, Beverly closed the door behind her and went down to meet Stan.

Chapter 25

Caterina watched the limousine pull off and then sneaked towards the back of the cottage. She had decided that the only way to free herself and save Mark, was to get some kind of evidence, something, to hold over Edward Chang. Blackmail had forced her into this life of deceit, perhaps it would free her from it as well.

She looked into the open window. The bed was unmade and she could hear the shower running. A man's trousers were draped over a woven straw chair. There was an envelope on the table beside the bed. Two of Toni's men had gone with her, Caterina assumed, to the airport. Her work was done. She had seemed satisfied by Mark's wallet, that her loose ends had been neatly clipped. That meant that only Larry remained, and he was in the shower.

Furtively, Caterina climbed through the window. The stiletto she held tightly in one hand, caught the sun and glimmered ominously. She hoped not to have to use it, but she would be a fool to try and go it unarmed. She detested guns, though she was adept at handling them. The stiletto was quick, quiet and deadly.

She dropped to the floor and made her way quickly to the table, picking up the envelope. The water was splashing in the other room and Larry was gargling some tune, unaware of any other presence. She opened the envelope. There was a thick wad of bills, an airline ticket and a slip of paper.

Pulling out the paper first, she stared in horror. The address of her family's home in Cuba was listed at the top. Beneath it was a description of her mother and two sisters. There was also a U.S. phone number and password jotted at the bottom of the page. Caterina pulled out the airline ticket. It was a round-trip ticket to Cuba, the flight leaving out tomorrow.

That bastard, Caterina thought. She had done everything Edward had asked of her, spied, seduced, stolen, carried drugs and drug money—all to save her family. And he was planning on killing them all anyway. She thought hard. If Edward planned to take her family out, that meant he was done with her as well, since they were his trump card. So he was planning on dispensing with her as well. Sending Larry, no doubt, to finish her before he caught his plane of death to Cuba.

The water in the shower was off. Caterina slipped behind the door, loosening her grip on the stiletto. She had no intention of allowing Edward to end the game this way. Larry opened the door of the bathroom and stepped out, a towel around his waist, another over his head as he toweled off his hair. Caterina moved quickly behind him, slipping the sharp, steel rod into his back, expertly piercing his heart.

Larry turned sharply, a look of surprise on his face as he saw Caterina standing there with the red-tipped weapon in her gloved hand. Surprise turned to anger and Larry took a step towards his holster, and then slumped to the floor, a small trickle of blood leaking out of the wound in his back.

Caterina stepped over him and studied his face. His eyes were open, and he looked insulted, as he realized at the last minute that his death was at the hand of this small, underestimated woman.

Caterina picked up the envelope and climbed out of the window, looking back once more. This would not end it, of course. Edward and Toni would have to be brought down. She knew she couldn't do it alone. She had no choice. She would have to go to Mark and tell him the truth. After they had tried to kill him, Caterina was certain he'd want revenge.

She realized, of course, that he might turn on her, hate her for her part in all of this. Placing her hand on her stomach and rubbing small circles around her belly, she decided she had no choice. She'd have to tell him and let the chips fall where they may. But first, she would go back to the apartments and give her father the money and a ticket away from here. This beautiful town was no longer a sanctuary, a place they were preparing for their family. That dream was dead. As long as Chang used Brazil as a hiding place, she was not safe. Whatever happened to her after this, she didn't want to leave papa here, in this foreign place, alone to die.

She slipped into the brush and headed back for town. Behind her, the birds chirped and a breeze blew through the trees surrounding the now utterly silent cottage.

Chapter 26

Beverly sat in the gate area waiting room, waiting for the flight to Detroit to board. She scanned the Philadelphia Inquirer distractedly, her mind reviewing the call from Dexter. She wondered if perhaps she had mistaken Dexter's 'when I get back." Mark might be with him on that flight from Brazil. He'd come home after all this time away, and she wouldn't be there to greet him.

She was excited too. The meeting with the Reislings, Doris' excitement about their new home, the potential happiness the new properties could bring to families nationwide. Beverly believed this was her great opportunity. There was no glass ceiling with Tierrasanta. Sure, she would have benefited financially, but money was never a big issue. She lived very comfortably and within her means. Stan had also assured her that Young was meeting her for dinner before the investors' meeting to present a package that would probably include a very large sign-on bonus.

"I'm telling you, Bev, it's Easy Street from here on in. You are a mover. Today proved it, and they need people like you on their team. You can bet they are going to make the pot sweet for you. Just remember who got you in."

The combination of worry about Mark and the excitement about Tierrasante, had Beverly's stomach churning. She needed a ginger ale. She looked around for Stan, who had gone off to make a call, but saw no sign of him. She was watching their bags, so she couldn't leave until he returned. She swallowed hard and tried to focus on the newsprint.

An article on the National page caught her eye. Newswired from Detroit, it was a piece about Michigan's gubernatorial primaries, and there was mention of Mount Clemens, one of Tierrasante's planned communities and the subject of the investors' meeting she and Stan were flying out to attend. It talked about the benefits the construction would bring to the Detroit community and also, that the breaking ground of St. Clemens was projected to secure someone named Richard Chase' nomination for the democratic ticket.

Beverly was tingling with anticipation. One of her projects was making news. They—Tierrasante—would be contributing to the community at large. This was something Beverly could live with. They were—patrons— of a sort, to the community, while providing housing and services to that community's elite. Beverly sat up proudly, she was about to embark on her life's dream.

Stan came over and sat down. "What are you looking so satisfied about?"

Beverly handed Stan the paper and pointed to the article. "Take a look at this. This article will make tonight's meeting a cakewalk. You know that if it made our papers, the news is all over the locals out there. People will be climbing the walls to get in. The rest of Detroit will throw a parade for the Heroes of Tierrasante. We're bringing in over 2,000 jobs on this project."

Stan scanned the paper and tossed it aside. "Mt. Clemens and the other communities are going to make us rich, Bev. It will make the residents of each of those communities feel happy and privileged and safe. And people will get some work. But don't go romanticizing Tierrasante, okay? It is a business. The jobs and all are just by-products of an extremely profitable venture. They don't care about those people, or the community, or us. They'd let people sleep on the streets if it were the more profitable to do so, and you and I would be out on our ears if they didn't think we were the best. They are looking out for their best interests and that's it. Don't forget that, Bev."

Beverly looked at Stan. "What's up with you? Why are you so pessimistic all of a sudden? I thought you were their biggest fan."

Stan looked away. "Let's just say, I have had the opportunity to see a bit more of Tierrasante than you have. It's a great opportunity and I intend to make the most of it, but I also recognize the reality of business. Okay? So just enjoy the ride, but always watch your back. Trust me on this one."

Beverly felt a chill run up her spine and shivered. Her stomach groaned its anxiety, and she remembered she needed that ginger ale. "I'm going to get something for my stomach. Want anything?"

Stan smiled bitterly, "Sure, Bev. I want the world."

Chapter 27

Mark stood by the window, his back turned to Caterina. She sat on the edge of the bed, her chin held bravely up, tears in her eyes.

"Mark, they threatened to kill my family. Can't you understand that? At first, you were nobody, just another American they wanted me to watch. You meant nothing to me, but my family is everything." She lowered her head and whispered softly, "I didn't know I would fall in love with you. Everything changed after that."

"They think you are dead. Your friend gave me your wallet, which I gave to Toni as proof of your death in the crash. I swear to you I didn't know about that—about your being the pilot, until after it had happened."

Mark turned to her, a sneer on his face. "You *swear* to me? You've been lying to me since the beginning, why should I believe you aren't setting me up now?"

Caterina's tears flowed freely. Through choked sobs she answered, "I'm not setting you up, Mark. I love you. They told me to find out if you'd really been killed, and if not, to finish the job. If I were setting you up, I would have killed you that night in the favela." She sighed.

"I don't blame you for hating me. But I had to do what I had to do. Anyway, you're free now. They think you are dead, so they won't come after you anymore."

Mark leaned against the window, his arms folded across his chest. "And you? Are you free now to go on to your next 'assignment'?"

Caterina lowered her head. "It's not like that, Mark. Not anymore. Not since I found you. But no, I'm not free. They had already decided to dispose of me and kill my family in Cuba. I won't be free until I get Edward Chang." She thought about Larry's face as he lay dead on the floor of the cottage. "I've only bought some time. Time enough, I hope, to get my father out of Ilhéus and into hiding."

Mark hardened his heart against Caterina's tears. "I have to get back to the States. Dexter and me will bring 'em down. No problem—easy day. This is just the kind of action I've been waiting for. As for you, good luck."

Mark bent down to pick up his bag. Just then, a tomato splashed against the window, and Mark rolled to the floor, then saw what it was. He stood against the wall and peeked out into the street. The fruit lady was standing below the window, staring up.

"Crazy old bag. What's up with her?" He turned back to Caterina, who was up and moving towards the door.

"We have to get out of here. She is a friend and watches out for us. That is a warning that danger is near."

Just then, Toni's two henchmen came around the corner in an open Jeep and pulled up in front of the building. The passenger had his gun drawn, there was another gun on the seat between them. Mark moved quickly, grabbing Caterina's hand, he pulled her out into the hall and headed for the stairs.

The two men burst into the lobby as Caterina and Mark raced down the steps. The first pointed a gun at them and they froze. It was as if in slow motion. The assailant's arm rose up, pointing the gun and then there was a shot. He fell to the ground in a pool of blood. Mark saw the old man behind the counter, smoke curling from the Colt .45 he held in his hand.

The second man turned and shot at the old man, as Caterina pulled a knife from her sleeve and threw it. It caught the man in the neck and he grappled at it as blood spurted. Caterina was across the floor and by her father's side, even as the man dropped his gun and fell to the floor. Taking the gun from her father's fingers and hugging him tightly, Caterina turned to Mark.

"We're out of time Mark. You'd better get out of here while you can."

The fruit lady came in the front door and looked at the two men dead on the floor. She said something to Caterina in rapid Portuguese. Caterina nodded and brought her father over to her. The fruit woman put her arm around the old man and Caterina kissed him before letting go and stepping back. As they made their way out the front door, the old man turned back to Caterina. "*Te quiero, mi niña*[5]."

Caterina stifled a sob as she answered, "*Si, Pepo. E yo...con mi alma*[6]."

When they were out the door and gone, Caterina sank to the floor. Mark came over to her and helped her up, then held her tightly. "Come on, love. We have to go."

Caterina looked up at him. "We?"

Mark smiled grimly. "Yes. We've got to get back to the States and put an end to this once and for all. I can't just sit here and wait until Dex contacts me. We'll have to take matters into our own hands and meet up with Dexter in Detroit." He put his arm around her waist and held her tightly.

---

5. I love you, my little girl.

6. "And you...with my soul."

Chapter 28

"So you'll be meeting Greg downstairs at the restaurant at six o'clock and we'll catch up around 7:45 P.M. to go over the presentation one last time."

Stan and Beverly stood just outside her hotel room door. He reached for Beverly's hand. "Listen, I'm sorry about my mood earlier. Too many things going on at once, I guess. This is a great opportunity, and I know you'll knock Greg out tonight. I'm glad you're getting in on this, Bev." He rushed on squeezing Beverly's hand, "I've made—I'll make—certain of that."

Beverly was concerned as she studied Stan's face and tried to withdraw her crushed hand. She forced a nonchalant smile. "It's fine, Stan. I understand about things getting under the skin." Her mind flashed to Dexter and Mark. She shook the thought away and focused back on Stan. "We're a team, deal?"

"Deal." Stan picked up his bag. "We have a little while before your meeting. Want to have a drink?"

Beverly shook her head. "I'll have to take a raincheck, okay? I need to make a few calls and maybe sneak in a quick nap before I get ready for dinner. Big night tonight and I want to be at my best."

Stan headed down the hall. "As if you are ever less. I'll catch up with you later then." He turned and walked down the hall a few yards and put his bags down in front of his door. Fishing for his key, he looked up and grinned as he watched Beverly slide the key through. She waved and walked in, closing the door behind her. Stan's smile faded once Beverly was gone, and with a sigh, went into his room and slipped the chain over the lock.

• • •

Beverly closed the door behind her, and smiled as she walked into the suite. It was lovely. Fresh cut flowers were arranged in bowls around the room, which was tastefully decorated French Colonial, which was upholstered in striped and floral patterns of yellow and blue. The lights on the end tables flanking the overstuffed sofa were on, lending a wonderfully soft glow to the room. There was a fireplace with a gilded screen and mirrored wet bar against the far wall. On it's gleaming counter was a basket overflowing with fruit, cheeses, chocolates, crackers and a bottle of Veuve Cliquot champagne, all done up with a huge red welcome bow and a card.

Putting her bags beside a blue moiré Queen Ann chair, Beverly kicked her shoes off and padded across the room to the basket. Plucking a sweet red grape into her mouth, she read the card. "Looking forward to dinner tonight and a mutually prosperous future. Greg." *Hmph*, she grinned. He was certainly sure of himself. But she had to admit, the man had style.

Nibbling on the grapes, Beverly picked up the phone and dialed her office. "Robin? Hi, it's Beverly Madsen. Did I get another call in from Mr. Racine?"

"I'm afraid not, Ms. Madsen."

"Oh. Okay. Well, were there any other calls?" Beverly asked, hoping against home that Mark might have phoned.

"All's quiet here, Ms. Madsen. But I have your information right next to the switchboard, just in case."

Thanks, Robin. Have a good evening." Beverly disconnected the call and then checked her answering machine. There were three messages. She listened impatiently as it ran through an invitation to dinner, Lauri letting her know she'd gotten the note, but was not giving it to 'that inconsiderate loser,' and her dentist's office, confirming her appointment. Nothing from Mark. Nothing from Dexter.

• • •

Dexter pushed his way through Customs and the crowds of sun tanned travelers milling in Miami's International Terminal. He had a two-hour layover before his flight into Detroit. After picking up the ticket, left as promised, by Bremmer, Dexter found a quiet corner and slumped into it, exhausted. The thought of boarding another plane, this time a three-hour flight, after sitting stuffed into the crowded plane from Ilhéus into São Paulo, followed by a seven hour flight into Miami, was overwhelming.

He thought he might try to catch a nap, but was too wired to doze. He realized he wouldn't be in Detroit until after 10:00 P.M., and by the time he got out of the airport and to the hotel, it would be too late to reach Beverly. He got up, stretched, and went to the phone. Maybe he could still catch her at the office.

Robin answered the phone. "Canterbury Associates, how may I direct your call?"

"Beverly Madsen, please. Dexter Racine calling."

"Oh, Mr. Racine! I'm *so* glad you called! Ms. Madsen left a message for you. Do you have a pen?"

Dexter pulled his pen out of his jacket and patted his pockets, looking for something to write on. His hand brushed the wallet Mark had given him, as he pulled out the envelope holding his boarding pass and flipped it over. "Go ahead."

"Ms. Madsen had a meeting in Detroit. She's staying at the Barrington, Room 761. I'll give you the number."

Dexter wrote it down. "Got it." He thanked Robin, hung up and dialed the hotel. "Room 761, please."

The phone rang six times, before the operator picked up again. "I'm sorry, the party is not answering. Would you like to leave a message?"

"Yes. This is Dexter Racine. Just got in from São Paulo and am flying in to Detroit this evening, on the 7:20 flight out of Miami, arriving Detroit 10:05. I'll try to reach her again before I board, otherwise, I am checking into the Hyatt and will call her around 11 P.M." Dexter paused. "Did you get that?"

"Yes sir." The operator repeated the message. Satisfied, Dexter added, "please make sure she gets this message as soon as possible. It is very urgent."

"Very good sir. Have a good evening."

Dexter hung up the phone and went back to his seat. Beverly was in Detroit. It seemed too good to be true. He was excited at the prospect of seeing her, and then sobered as he remembered why they had to meet.

He remembered the wallet in his pocket and decided to take a look at it. Maybe there would be something in it that would help Dexter somehow explain why Mark could not return to the States. Something to tell Beverly that would make the blow less harsh. There was a computer disk tucked in the bill fold.

He opened his laptop and waited for it to power up. He slipped in the disk, and after scanning it's contents for a few minutes, hit upon information that shocked him.

He was looking at what appeared to be a working file. The first document Dexter opened was a detailed report on a land development outside of Detroit, called Mount Clemens. There was a memo with account numbers which Dexter recognized as bank ABA numbers used to wire transfer funds between a bank in Brazil and one in Detroit. The memo was written to someone named Edward, from "Toni."

Every trace of fatigue left Dexter as he scanned the file. *This could be big*, Dexter thought. He closed the memo and tried to open another file. It was encrypted. One by one, he tried unsuccessfully to open the other files. He hit the keyboard in frustration. He had seen enough. Maybe it meant nothing, maybe it would help Mark. He had to get those files opened. Dexter removed the disk and rushed to the phones, putting a call in to Bremmer's cell phone. He caught him in his car.

Bremmer picked up. "Yeah, Bremmer."

"It's Dexter. I need your help on something. I have this disk that may identify possible drug money laundering from Brazil. Unfortunately, the files are encrypted. I need you to have someone decode it so you can take a more thorough look. I'll FedEx the disk to you before I get on the plane, you'll get it first thing in the morning. I gotta run, my flight leaves in about an hour. I'll be at the hotel by 11 p.m."

"How the hell did you get the disk? How do you know it's legit?"

"I don't know—just the one memo I could open, but I got the disk from a credible source who came upon it...fortuitously. That's why I'm sending it to you. If it is, we've been given an early Christmas present. It's certainly worth looking into.

"Listen, I am also sending an international driver's license along. I need you to track it down, see if it connects with this."

"Can do easy. If you're right...I'll be in the office first thing in the morning and have a nutcracker ready to go as soon as the envelope arrives. I'll call you as soon as I find out what we've got." "Thanks, I'll call you from Detroit."

Chapter 29

"Sir, Mr. Chase' assistant has informed that he is not available. He said Chase would have to get back to you."

Chang gripped the phone, furious. That piece of shit. How dare Chase blow him off? He was perfectly aware that Chase was in his suite, had been for the past two hours. "Get me Toni, NOW." He slammed down the phone.

Young had just raked Edward over the coals because of the Brazilian issue. It made him look incompetent, this slip up of Toni's. Just when he was on the brink of greatness, someone missed a detail, made an error and Edward was blamed. And now, Chase was not taking his calls.

Chang clenched his fists in an effort to quell the fury rising up in him. Good news from the Michigan front might have offset some of Young's anger, but now Chase was "unavailable."

"Well," Edward laughed aloud as he rocked back on his heels, "I will have to handle everything myself." It was clear to him that no one had the heart, the courage or the brilliance that he possessed. He was willing and able to do whatever was necessary to reach his goals. He would not be denied—not ever again would he be denied his rightful place at the top. Chang's face clouded with rage, as his thoughts moved back to Chase.

Just who did Chase think he was dealing with? If he thought he could just blow him off like a piece of lint from his suit, he was seriously mistaken. *I own that prick.* Chase was stamped "paid." He'd have to remind Chase of just who was running this show.

Suddenly, Edward made a decision. His destiny was not going to be compromised. He would find out about the pilot, Mark by any means necessary, and then he would deal with Chase. One way or the other, Edward intended to solve all of his problems once and for all.

• • •

Beverly and Stan sat in a booth in the back of the crowded restaurant. Beverly ran her finger around the rim of her wineglass and watched worriedly as Stan tossed back a second very dry Martini in a single gulp.

"I've never seen you like this, Stan. You're scaring me. Now tell me what's going on? You've been edgy all day."

"It's nothing I can't handle, Bev." He smiled, slightly inebriated. "In fact, I have handled it. Stan the Man is on the j-o-b, though there are those who might underestimate him."

Beverly pushed her glass aside and leaned her elbows on the table. "Listen to me, Stan. We're a team right? And if one of us is having a problem, we both have a problem. Maybe I can help—try me."

Stan motioned for the waitress. "Bring me another. Make this one a double—and put two olives in it for good luck." He smiled again at Beverly, and pointed at her.

"You are good, Bev. I'll give you that. But I have this one under—"he hiccuped, "control. Believe me, it won't do you any good to prod me, I won't tell, unless I have to. And now, Stan-the-Man will smoothly change the subject. How's—"

Beverly looked up, cutting off Stan's words and nodded towards the entrance. "Look—Greg Young just walked in. Pull it together."

Young had entered with several other men. As they were being escorted to their table, Young looked up and caught Beverly's eye. He smiled and excused himself from his party, making his way over to their table.

"He's on his way over to our table. Are you alright?"

"I'm jesh…fine," Stan slurred. "Don't you worry your pretty little head about me." He sat up straighter, adjusting his tie. It now lay slanted across his shirt.

Beverly looked up and smiled. "Gregory, what a pleasant surprise. Would you care to join us?"

Young glanced at the red-rimmed eyes of Stan and his lips tightened imperceptibly. He looked back at Beverly and smiled. "Thank you. But I can only stay for a moment."

Beverly slid over, so Young could sit beside her. He glanced again at Stan and then back to Beverly. "I understand you closed your first deal for Tierrasante this morning. That's what I like, a real go-getter. We are going to do wonderful things together, Ms. Madsen. Are you ready to take on the world?"

Stan leaned forward. "Of course, we're ready. We are professionals." He leered at Young, "but are you? Are you ready?"

Young's eyes narrowed as he addressed Stan, "Mr. Towers, I can assure you, I do what is necessary to get the job done."

He turned back to Beverly. "I'm looking forward to our dinner later. We have a lot to discuss. One of my executives, Edward Chang, will be joining us. He is the head of operations here on the Mt. Clemens project and someone I think you'll need to know. But we have to get you aboard. Here you are already earning commissions and we haven't even ironed out all the details"

Stan interrupted them, leaning forward, "I am sure you'll iron out all the details, *Mr.* Young, that is, all the details within your control. But you may find that you don't have everything under your control, Greg-o. That's right. You don't know as much as you'd like to think you know."

Beverly was horrified at Stan's outburst. "Stan, what has gotten into you?"

Young smiled at Beverly, "That's alright, Ms. Madsen. I can see that Stan is not…shall I say…quite with us just now." He turned to Stan. His eyes were cold, but his voice did not betray anything—for Beverly's sake.

"Stan, I understand you are under some pressure right now, so I'll forgive that outburst. I will also see to it that we get things wrapped up here as quickly as possible," he turned to Beverly and smiled, "so we can relieve some of this tension."

He stood. "Now, I mustn't keep my party waiting any longer. Ms. Madsen, we'll talk tonight."

He turned to Stan and with a curt nod said, "Stan." Then he turned on his heel and walked quickly away.

"Isn't he the debonair gentleman? 'I mustn't keep my party waiting.'" Stan snorted.

"Stan, I don't know what's eating you , but you'd better pull it together. I suggest you get back to your room, take a long shower and sleep it off. I've never seen you like this, and frankly, I don't like it."

Beverly's tone softened, "Anyway, I have to get upstairs too. I want to go over the files before our meeting tonight. Why don't I drop you at your room?"

Stan stood unsteadily. "I'm sorry, Bev. I'll just splash my face and get it together. Then I'll drop you off at your room, like a proper gentleman. Excuse me."

Stan wound his way unsteadily to the men's room and disappeared inside. Beverly slumped back in her chair with a sigh. *What the devil was going on with him?*

Chapter 30

Dexter dropped his bags by the door and sat on the edge of the bed. He looked around and sighed. He wished, for a moment, that he had never gotten involved in this mess. In the past few days, his life had been completely turned inside out. He'd gotten first a call from Beverly, after months of silence, asking him to find Mark. That call had been followed almost immediately by another call, this time Mark's mother, Mrs. Davis, asking him to go to Brazil to claim his body. And he'd flown to Brazil, expecting the worst—and had found his best friend battered, but alive and living with another woman.

Dexter smiled ruefully. Maybe he had found "the worst" after all. Even as he worried about how he would tell Beverly that Mark was gone from her life, Mark had handed him a story of intrigue and attempted murder. And now, after fifteen hours on planes, he was sitting in Detroit, for heaven's sake—searching for a woman who carried false papers, in the *hopes* that she might be here. And if he did find her, then what?

Mark and his cowboy dreams. If the woman was here in Detroit, what could he do? Walk up to her and say, "*Pardon me, ma'am, you don't know me. Heck, I don't know you either—but a friend found this license after that helicopter crash in Brazil. You know the one, the one that perhaps you arranged? Would you mind confessing to everything, or better yet, why don't you just go on back down to Brazil so my best friend can mete out the justice he thinks is due him. You did, after all, almost kill him."*

Maybe he'd arrest her for carrying marked up helicopter manuals—intent to learn schematics? The best plan, though, was probably to just turn her name and address over to Mark, so he could come barreling into the hotel with his pearl-handled six-shooters drawn.

He pulled the license out of this jacket pocket and studied the picture. She was a good looking woman, he had to admit. But taking a phony card and accepting that the address on it *might* be right, was too far a stretch for his intelligence-trained imagination. It just couldn't happen.

Tossing the card aside, Dexter stood and stretched. Well, he would give it his best shot. He had promised Mark that much. But first, at the very least, he needed a long, hot shower, a good meal, maybe a drink and a nap. As he pulled his tie off and tossed it on the bed, Dexter reordered his priorities. A short, hot shower, and a nap.

• • •

The hotel lobby was noisy and loud, when Dexter came down, mildly refreshed from his nap. He pushed his way over to the restaurant, and found that without a reservation, he would have at least a 45 minute wait. The hostess wrote his name down on the list and directed him to the bar. "We'll call you as soon as a table becomes available, Mr. Racine."

Dexter sat at the bar and ordered a drink. *What am I doing?* He wondered as he absently stirring the ice around his glass. A woman noticed him sitting there and approached him.

"Cheer up, it's a party." The woman slid on to the bar stool beside him.

Dexter turned to her and smiled, "Don't let me ruin the atmosphere."

She grazed his shoulder with her long, manicured nails and leaned closer to him. "That's hardly possible dear. Are you here for the convention?"

Dexter shrugged, "It seems I'm the only one who's not."

The woman's hand lingered on Dexter's arm, "Well then, are you here for business or pleasure?"

Dexter looked into the mirror behind the bar and noticed a woman standing at a table behind him, looking bored as her companion talked loudly about the election, the state of the country and the good old days. She looked up and saw him studying her. Her face silently asked him to rescue her. He nodded slightly and got up from the stool, turning to the woman beside him.

"If you'll excuse me, I think it's time for me to cast a vote."

The woman followed Dexter's glance at the woman at the table and then smiled slightly at Dexter. "Your prerogative, but just remember—one man, one vote."

Dexter nodded and excused himself. He walked up to the couple and said, "Ms. Taylor, the Committee Chairman would like a word with you." He put his hand on the small of her back, and with a nod towards her companion, ushered her away.

The woman turned to Dexter, "Thanks. Do you always rescue women in dire straits?"

Dexter bowed slightly. "Only when they inspire me. I'm Racine. Dexter Racine."

The woman studied Dexter appreciatively. "Dexter Racine. Nice name. I'm Karen Taylor, but I guess you knew that already. I don't remember seeing you at the Simmons staff luncheon."

Dexter winked at Karen pointing to her convention badge. "Who's Simmons?"

Karen laughed, "You must be from out of town. I assumed you were here for the convention. Neil Simmons is the mayor of Detroit and is in the middle of the most heated gubernatorial race this state has ever seen. He's running against the former Lt. Governor, Richard Chase. Don't you watch the news?"

Dexter grinned, "Isn't that on during Seinfield?"

Karen punched his arm lightly, laughing. "That's a good one. Then what brings you here to Detroit?"

Before Dexter could answer, there was a great deal of commotion. A moment later, Governor Roberts walked into the bar with his entourage. The DJ stopped the music for a moment and announced his arrival.

Toni entered with them, but in the confusion, stepped away from the group and went over to the booths lining the walls. Dexter watched her as she moved across the room, looking quickly over her shoulder as she slid into the booth, joining two men already seated there having drinks. Dexter turned back to Karen.

"Who's that?" He nodded in Toni's direction.

Karen glanced at Toni and waved her hand dismissively. That's Toni Moore. She's the financial consultant for the Chase' campaign. Why? Interested?"

Dexter turned back to Karen, taking her hand. "I'm only interested in knowing what you're doing for dinner tomorrow?"

Karen smiled up at Dexter. "Is that an invitation?" She caught movement in her peripheral vision and turned, "Uh oh, this is going to be good. That's the mayor."

Simmons and his staff walked into the club, surrounded by a cache of reporters. Governor Roberts walked over to the mayor, shaking his hand. As they posed for the flashing bulbs of the reporters' cameras, someone shouted, "Hey—turn up the volume."

Everyone turned to the television over the bar at the news report.

"This is an Eyewitness News election week update. With only two days until the Democratic primaries, former Lt. Governor Richard Chase' office has announced that the governor has approved the construction of Mount Clemens Village, a Canterbury Residential development. If successful, it is estimated that the Canterbury development will bring over two thousand jobs and one billion dollars to the suburban communities surrounding Detroit. In a surprise move, the governor, with the same stroke of pen, disapproved Detroit's five million dollar education grant to update the City's school system. Today's decisions by the governor's office will further divide this race along racial lines, but polls are showing that Chase' has secured a significant lead over Mayor Simmons in the bid for the governor's mansion."

The reporters all turned to the Governor and Simmons, pens and cameras poised. Simmons glared at the Governor, at a loss for words. The Governor smiled sheepishly, aware of the lights and cameras pointed at him. Suddenly, the reporters moved in, shouting questions. Simmons clenched his fists in anger and then smoothed his face to a look of deep concern and regret. He addressed the reporters, careful to step just right of the Governor, to ensure that the cameras would pick up his reaction. He raised his hands to silence the reporters.

"As mayor of this City, I have had the opportunity to witness a period of growth, preside over a plethora of graduations, building dedications, christenings and have had the honor of serving on many important local and national committees as a representative of the people. I have also had the unpleasant responsibility of consoling loved ones and survivors of fallen policemen, firemen and citizens of this great state. I have had to find the words to let them know why we, as Michiganders, grieved with them, and why such a horrible price had to be paid. There was never a sufficient answer, especially for life lost to crime."

He paused, looking dramatically troubled as the cameras flashed. "I am going to make a prediction today, folks. I predict—Tom, Barbara—are you getting this all down?

"I predict that this man," he pointed accusingly at the governor, "will murder thousands of children and will commit over thirty thousand people to poverty in the next generation."

The bar, silent until now, erupted in excitement and movement, as everyone moved in closer to stare at the murdering governor. His staff moved into place around him, keeping the people away from him as they searched out an exit path. Simmons went on, his voice rising ministerially.

"We ought to arrest him now! The Governor of this state has sentenced the children of Detroit to a life of poverty, crime and unemployment today,. This man, in whom these poor children's parents placed their trust and their children's' futures. Worse than that, they will probably never achieve the basic functioning skills to understand why! Let's talk about crime. This is a crime, and I pray…"

Simmons pulled out a handkerchief and dabbed his forehead, and then turned to the Governor. "I pray that ten years from now, one of those lost children don't mistake you, Governor, or your family, for an everyday working citizen and bash your head in for a dollar bill. That is what you have sentenced them to."

The reporters shouted questions at the Governor, who declined to answer as his bodyguards ushered him out of the bar, pushing aside the crowds. Simmons answered some of the reporters' questions and allowed a few more photographs to be taken.

Finally, his people ushered him out of the bar as well.

Karen shook her head. "This is big. Chase settled Mount Clemens. Dexter, I'm going to have to leave you—" She turned around, but Dexter was gone.

Chapter 31

Beverly turned her head in the direction of a sudden burst of animated noise spilling from the bar and then turned her attention back to the conversation at her table. "A lot of excitement going on out there."

Young took a sip of his wine. "Yes, well the Democratic convention is in a few days, so the place is filling up with political rowdies from around the state. Now, Beverly, where were we? You were telling me you'd review our offer and give me an answer tomorrow morning?"

Beverly placed her napkin on the table. "Yes. As I mentioned, I do have some lingering issues with leaving Canterbury so precipitously, but it is a wonderful opportunity and certainly bears serious consideration."

"Wonderful. I want to apologize that Mr. Chang was not able to join us. We have some pressing matters with Mt. Clemens that needed immediate attention."

"I understand." Beverly took a sip of her coffee. "Actually, Mt. Clemens came up in a discussion with a friend earlier today, though I can't say it was in a favorable circumstance."

"Really? What did you hear?"

"The name came up in a conversation on another matter. A close friend of mine was nearly killed in a helicopter crash in Brazil a few days ago, and Mount Clemens was mentioned." Beverly paused, Mark's face flashing across her mind. She shook her head and smiled apologetically. "It's a long story and I don't have all the details, so I won't bore you with it."

Young stirred his coffee with a studied calm, "No, please, do tell us what you do know. It always amazes me how people hear about our projects, especially one that is not yet public knowledge—and all the way from Brazil...I'm fascinated."

Beverly took a deep breath. "Well, it seems there was a woman who was involved in the accident I mentioned. Well, it seems she was actually responsible for the accident. My friend managed to get some information from her, which indicated that she was from the Detroit area and that she was somehow connected with Mount Clemens. As I said, the details are a little sketchy—I'm sure she isn't really connected with Tierrasante, but the name did come up. Interesting, isn't it?" Beverly chuckled self-consciously.

Young smiled. "Yes, well, I am certain this woman had no connection to our project. Certainly I would know about that, no? Anyway, I am pleased to hear that your friend was not killed, Beverly. That certainly gives the story a happy ending."

Young looked at his watch and then took his napkin from his lap and placed it on the table. "Well, Beverly, this has certainly been delightful and I want to say again, that I hope you will give our offer serious thought. We offer unlimited opportunity for the right person. In any event, I have an overseas conference call scheduled before the investor's meeting this evening, so I will have to leave you now."

He pulled out a gold engraved case and removed a business card, handing it to Beverly. "If you have any questions or concerns before the meeting, or about the offer letter, don't hesitate to call me. Otherwise, until tonight?"

Beverly smiled as she took the card. "Looking forward. And Edward, thank you." She shook his hand.

Young quickly departed. Beverly sat back and watched him go. She'd wanted to scream "yes!" to the generous offer Young had laid out for her, but she didn't forget her business head. *Never seem too eager.* She'd wait the requisite hours, listen in on the investors' meeting and then call in the morning to accept the deal.

Chapter 32

The phone rang, jerking Stan out of an alcohol-induced sleep. He grabbed for the receiver before it could ring again. "Stan Towers."

"Did I wake you, Stan?" It was Young

Stan shook his head. He was groggy, and struggled to sound alert. "No ...no, of course not. I was just reviewing my notes from the meeting so I could get a report to you first thing in the morning. Is there something I can do for you?"

"As a matter of fact, there is. Beverly told me a fascinating story this evening regarding her fiancé, the one who was almost killed in Brazil. I'm sure you know the story. What was his name?"

Stan sat back, "Mark, sir. Mark Davis."

"Ah, yes. Mr. Davis." Young paused, as if gathering his thoughts. When he spoke again, his voice was brisk. It echoed through Stan's pounding head, sending a wave of nausea through him. "Stan, I need to know where Mr. Davis is, how to get in touch with him. It is a matter of some urgency."

Stan's head suddenly cleared. "Has something happened to Beverly?"

"No, of course not. We had a lovely dinner, talked...she is, no doubt, in her suite reviewing our offer package and preparing for this evening's meeting. I simply need to know where I can get in touch with Mark."

"Well, uh, I wouldn't have that information, Greg. He's in the service and travels a lot, but I haven't even met him yet." Stan paused, adding cautiously, "I'm sure Beverly wouldn't mind telling you how to reach him. Why don't you give her a call?"

"This is actually a rather sensitive situation, Stan. For reasons I don't care to go into right now, I would prefer not to go directly to Beverly on this. That," "is why I am asking you to find out. And I need the information immediately."

"Sir, if you don't mind, may I ask why you need to reach him? I'm certain Beverly will ask me the same question."

"That, Mr. Towers, is why I am depending on your discretion. I cannot reveal the purpose of this errand I am charging you with. Just understand that it must be done, done quickly, and you must find a way to get that information to me, without alerting Beverly to who is asking for it."

Stan stared out of the window, his heart pounding in his chest. *Jeez. If I keep doing this, I'll have a stroke before I'm forty.* "Very well, sir. I have to say, I am uncomfortable doing this, but I'll give Beverly a call. I will let you know if I find out anything."

Young's voice was menacing as he said, "I cannot emphasize enough, how strongly I suggest that you *do* get that information. Your life could depend on it, Mr. Towers. Do I make myself clear?"

Stan could feel sweat tracing down his spine as he nodded, "Perfectly."

Young's voice relaxed. "Good. Then I'll expect a call from you with that information."

"Fine. I mean, yes *Sir.*

• • •

Beverly stepped from the shower and wrapped herself in the luxurious robe provided by the hotel. Sitting on the edge of her bed, she massaged avocado butter into her skin and then went to the bureau, selected one of the perfumes she'd brought along, and dotted the scented drops at her pulse points. This was an important meeting for her.

It was clear that joining Tierrasante would catapult her and her career into the big leagues, where she'd dreamed of being since she was a business major in college.

Beverly pulled on sheer, gray stockings and a silky black slip. It always made her feel more confident when she wore soft lingerie under her business suit. Silly, she supposed, but there it was. Nothing made her feel more in control than a lovely tap set or lacy slip under her take-no-prisoner suits.

In fact, she considered, the gray tweed was both stunning and sophisticated on her. She wanted to look the picture of success to mark this new beginning.

When she finished dressing, she gave Stan a call. The phone rang three times and she was about to hang up, when he picked up the line. His voice sounded a strained, "Hello?"

"Stan, it's Bev. I thought we'd grab a cup of coffee downstairs and review the game plan one more time." Beverly smiled. "*And,* I want to tell you about my meeting with Greg."

There was a long pause, and then Stan said, "I'm…uh…I'm running a little late, Bev. Why don't you go on down and order those coffees. I'll join you as soon as I can."

"Are you alright, Stan? You sound a little strange."

Stan's voice was muffled as he answered, "I have a few things on my mind, Bev. But as soon as I take care of them, I'm sure I'll be just fine."

Stan went into the bathroom and splashed cold water on his face. Grabbing a towel, he looked into the mirror and thought, *This is really no big deal. So he wants to know about Beverly's fiancé. Probably just wants more insight into Beverly. It really is reasonable, if you think about it.*

But Stan had thought about it, and it didn't sound reasonable to him. It didn't sound innocent or completely honest, either. He would get the information Young wanted, but when he got back to Philadelphia, Stan intended to put his insurance policy into effect.

Chapter 33

Chang thought about the years he'd spent hustling on the streets of Hong Kong, before a high ranking, local drug underking who took him under his wing had noticed him. He'd traded numbers and nickel bags for custom-tailored suits and a beeper, as he was promoted to personal bodyguard. In this world, it finally didn't matter that he was half American, in fact, it had been his ticket in. His command of English and his ability to move unseen among the white tourists and businessmen who teemed in the streets, made his an asset to the greedy drug lord, who had visions of expanding his small empire.

Chang had served as translator at many of the important meetings between his boss and American and European businessmen, and it was at one of those meetings that he met Mr. Young. His first assignment from Mr. Young had been the elimination of his old boss. He dispatched his duties without a moment of remorse. That had bought his ticket to the States.

Mr. Young had recognized early, the young Edward's genius and had sent him to school. He bought his ticket into Harvard, but Chang had earned his place at Wharton, graduating the highly competitive program at the top of his class.

With these victories, Chang had been given greater responsibility, but still felt that his value was not appreciated fully. When it was announced that the Michigan governor would not be running for office again, Chang decided to make his move. He would put a puppet into that office and expand Young's Colonnade project from there. This coup would be the first of many political alliances Edward would effect.

Young had been skeptical of his plan. *Too risky, forget it,* Young had determined. But Edward knew that this victory would assure his rightful place at the very top of the Tierrasante organization, of which, Chang sneered, Young was a small cog. He'd persuaded Young to let him approach the former Lt. Governor, Richard Chase with an offer. When he'd been more than eager to accept the funds Chang offered, Young approved the deal.

Chang had installed Toni, his lover and one of Detroit's best financial analyst into a key position on the campaign and she served as Chang's eyes and ears on the inside. They had to work around their responsibilities to Tierrasante, but they'd almost done it. The polls showed Chase in the lead, in the days before the democratic convention.

And then he sent Toni down to Ilhéus for more funds and all hell had broken loose. She'd used a pilot outside of their organization and had allowed him to escape. Now he was out there, a very real threat to everything Chang was working on, and he had no intention of letting anything get in his way.

As Chang pondered the situation, his eye caught the television, which stood in the corner of the room, it's sound muted. The screen blinked "Election Updates" and Chang turned up the volume as he poured another drink.

"Today, the race for Governor intensified in several states. But with all the fanfare normally associated with a primary, none has generated more attention than the race for Chief Executive of Michigan. With the continuing redistribution of the Michigan workforce to warmer and more prosperous regions, wheat production shortfalls, steady increases in urban crime, the race in Michigan is what some analysts are calling 'the first domino which will determine the fate of Middle America.' RBS corre-spondent, Danny O'Neill brings us the story from Detroit."

"Larry, the climate here in the Great Lakes State is brutal. The race involves two democratic camps, that of former Lieutenant Governor Richard Chase, and Detroit's two-term mayor, Neil Simmons. The mudslinging began earlier this year when Chase was quoted as describing Detroit as 'a drain on the state's coffers.' Mayor Simmons accused now Democrat governor Stu Roberts of withholding over five million dollars in much needed highway and educational funds, in an attempt to aid Richard Chase in his bid for Governor. Governor Roberts held a press conference earlier today denying charges of any impropriety and suggested Mayor Simmons spend more time balancing Detroit's budget, and less flying around the State raising campaign funds.

"Mayor Simmons has countered that Chase' campaign chest has swollen to over $4 million dollars in recent months, despite Chase's lack of fundraising appearances. Simmons is calling for an investigation into Simmons' funding sources. Sources inside the Chase' camp say the charges are unfounded and, I quote, 'a scurrilous attempt to divert attention from the pressing issues at hand.' This is an ugly campaign, Larry, and it will only get more controversial as we move towards the Democratic convention, convening here in Detroit next Tuesday. You can be sure that RBS News will be there for full coverage. This is Danny O'Neill, RBS News, Detroit."

The telephone rang. Chang picked it up. "Yes," he answered curtly.

"It's Young. Call me back on a secure line." The phone went dead.

Adrenaline pumped through Chang's body as he moved to his briefcase and took out his phone. He dialed Young's number. Young picked up on the first ring.

"We have a problem. That pilot your girlfriend used in Brazil is still alive."

Chang sighed in relief. "Mr. Young, I just spoke with Toni moments ago, and she has assured me that the pilot was killed in the helicopter crash."

"Oh really? Well I hope so. Because I just had lunch with a lovely lady, who happens to be that pilot's fiancée. *She* informs me that not only is her love still alive, but that he has mentioned Mount Clemens and a woman who might be involved, who lives in Detroit."

Chang's heart stopped. "Who is this woman?"

Young's voice was quietly menacing. "Her name is Beverly Madsen, a corporate real estate pro we are bringing in to the project. That is, if you haven't screwed it up with your incompetence."

Chang's voice shook as he answered, "Mr. Young, I can assure you that there is no problem. The project is secure."

"Well, it better be. Because if that pilot shows up alive, *you* my dear Edward, will show up dead. Am I understood?"

"Perfectly sir. I am on it."

"I certainly hope so, Edward. For your sake, I certainly hope so."

Chang picked up his drink and took a long swallow, trying to still the rage that shook his body. If it were true that that pilot were still alive, it could mess up everything he had been working for.

Chapter 34

"I'll take one of the helicopters and fly us to Salvador. We'll get a flight from there to Rio and on to Detroit. I know that woman is the key to all of this."

Mark and Caterina moved swiftly around the chain link fence that surrounded Sabo's airstrip.

"Mark—I think that—" Caterina's words were cut short by a quick hand motion from Mark.

There were two well dressed European men questioning Sabo's assistant, Antonio.

"They work for Toni," Caterina whispered.

"Dex was right. They're on to us."

Just then, one of the men grabbed Antonio's shoulder. They started struggling and Antonio kicked him in the jaw and then swung his leg around, kicking the second man in the leg. He yelled angrily in pain and grabbed Antonio's arm, twisting it behind his back. The first man punched Antonio in the stomach, and then the two men dragged him into the hangar.

Mark grabbed on to the fence and started to climb over. Caterina pulled him back. "What do you think you're doing? They'll make certain you are dead this time!"

The two men came out of the hangar alone, walking calmly, but swiftly, away from the building. As they climbed into their car and pulled away, the hangar exploded, the backlash throwing Mark from the fence and into the bushes. Sabo ran out on the tarmac waving his hands and screaming as he watched his building burn to the ground.

Caterina rushed over to Mark. He spit blood, and started to get up. "Those bastards. I'm going to…"

"Shhh. Mark, you are bleeding. Lay still. There is nothing we can do for Antonio now."

Mark pushed Caterina's hand away and stood, brushing himself off. "I'm fine," he growled as he stared at the hangar fire, watching the bright flames turn to black smoke.

"Fine…alright. What do we do now, cowboy?"

Mark turned and brushed past her, heading for the Jeep. "It's show time."

• • •

Caterina raced after Mark and hopped in the car as Mark pulled off, throwing up a cloud of dust in his wake. He raced towards the road the two men had taken. Caterina held on for dear life, screaming over the sound of the engine, "Mark! Mark! What are you doing?"

Mark, his face set in grim lines, just kept driving. Caterina looked over her shoulder at the receding line of the airstrip, and grabbed the wheel of the Jeep, turning it sharply. The Jeep careened off the road and crashed into a bank of bushes in the ravine.

In a rage, Mark raised his hand, as if to punch the windshield, but Caterina was in her own rage. She caught his wrist and yelled at him, "What do you think you're doing?"

She held on to his arm. "Do you think you can take them on, Cowboy? They have an army here. Do you hear me? An army. You go chasing after them and they will mow you down. Now, if you want to get them, we have to get to the States and get Chang and Toni, like we planned. We don't have much time. The Policia Militar will be out at Sabo's strip at any moment. If we don't get out of here now, we will not get out of here, because you can be certain they will arrest us."

Mark stared straight ahead, breathing hard, gritting his teeth. Caterina put her hand lightly on his arm and continued softly, "Mark, I love you. I don't want to lose you. I want revenge too. They hurt your pride, but they have destroyed my life. They threaten my family. Believe me, I want them all dead. But even more than that, I want to live. And that means, we have to get out of here."

Mark turned to Caterina, his face set and angry. He stared at her for a moment, and then sighed, as he reached out and touched her cheek gently. "You're right, amor. But I'll be damned if they're going let them ruin Bahia. I'll be back." He put the Jeep in reverse and pulled out of the ravine. After turning the Jeep around, he turned to her again, smiling slightly.

"But you almost killed us just now. You are going to have to find a better way of getting my attention in the future, okay?"

Chapter 35

Dexter rushed out to the lobby and headed for the phone banks. The place was still packed with people rushing about, arms filled with flyers and placards. Everyone was abuzz with the news of the confrontation between the mayor and the governor. The phones were all occupied. He had to get a hold of Mark. The woman was here!

He could hardly believe it. Dexter had not thought anything would come of his chase out to Detroit for Mark, and now, not only had he found the mystery woman, but she was in the midst of a controversial campaign, one where one of Beverly's projects played a decisive role. And what did any of this have to do with Brazil? Dexter had to get more information.

Pushing his way outside, he pulled out his cell phone and dialed the number Mark had given him. The phone rang twice, and then a mechanical voice came on, speaking in Portuguese. *Must be his service,* Dexter intuited, as he waited impatiently for the universal "leave message" beep. When it sounded, Dexter talked fast.

"Man, I need to get with you. I've seen your friend, need connection information. I'm at the Hyatt waiting on your call." Dexter disconnected the line. He'd try the number again in a few minutes, just to make certain it went through. He dialed Beverly's office number next.

"Canterbury Associates, how may I direct your call?"

"Beverly Madsen, please. Dexter Racine calling."

"I'm sorry, but Ms. Madsen is out of the office now. May I take a message?"

"Is she expected in later?"

"I'm afraid I don't have that information sir, but I can take a message. She will check in."

Dexter sighed in frustration. "Just tell her I called, Dexter Racine. It is urgent that I talk with her. She can reach me at the Hyatt in Detroit. I am waiting for her call. Got that?"

"Yes sir. I'll make sure she gets the message."

Dexter disconnected and put the phone back in his pocket. There was nothing more he could do at the moment, but wait. He headed back into the hotel, and went up to his room.

His phone was blinking, there was a message for him. Dexter peeled off his jacket and sat on the edge of the bed. He pressed the button. It was a call from Bremmer, demanding that he call the office immediately.

Dexter called down to the operator. "This is Dexter Racine in Room 871. I am expecting two very urgent calls. If they come in while I am on the line, I am to be interrupted."

"Very well, sir. I'll make a note."

Dexter called Bremmer's number. "This is Dex. What's going on?"

Bremmer's voice boomed through the receiver. "What do you mean, what's going on? Why the hell didn't you check in when you got into town?"

"I had some business to follow up on here, first. I thought I was in the office tomorrow, first thing."

"If you had checked it, hot shot, you'd have heard the news. Heads rolled this morning."

"What's going on?"

"Albans wants a rehash of the Tanaka visit. He's back in town, man."

"Tanaka? I thought they extradited him in '87."

"So did I. Evidently he's back and muscling around the Hill again. We have photos of him with the Speaker."

"Bob, you know we can't touch him as long as he's making rounds with the Speaker. Did Albans reopen it?"

"Not this time. He doesn't want to put any weight behind it, too controversial. But it is suspected that he has his pudgy little fingers in the Detroit elections. We don't have the connection yet, but when Albans heard you were up there, he blew a casket. You aren't working this without letting your old friend in on it, are you?"

"Completely unrelated matter, man. I am looking into something for that friend in Brazil. But," Dexter lowered his voice, "there might be a connection between this Detroit thing and Brazil. I don't know what it is yet, but I intend to find out."

"Do you need any help?"

"I don't think so, like I said, I'm not sure it has anything to do with any of our work, but it's a favor for a friend, so I need to dig a bit more." Dexter had an idea.

"Actually, you *could* do me a favor. I need you to get the feedback on that international license I gave you ASAP. I have a sneaking suspicion that she, is at the center of whatever is going on here. Find out who the artist is too—it could be one of our regulars. Also, I saw the woman on the license here in Detroit. Her real name is Toni Daniels. Would you run a quick check on her?"

"No prob. And I'll cover for you with Albans until Monday. But you get back here and keep your nose clean out there. If you find any connection between Tanaka and your errand, back off and call in. Understand?"

"I hear you. Give me a call when you have something for me." Dexter paused. "And thanks. I owe you."

"Damn right you do. And don't think I won't call it in sometime. Later."

Dexter hung up the phone and lay back on the bed, folding his arms under his head. So Tanaka was back on the Hill. The information niggled in the back of his mind. Somehow, that information was a piece of the puzzle—so was this Toni Daniels and, Dexter worried, somehow, Beverly was mixed up with this mess as well. Dexter moved the pieces around in his head, trying to make some sense of it all, but there wasn't enough information.

He sat up and pulled out a pen. On a piece of hotel stationary, he wrote notes:
Beverly—real estate—Tierrasante—Colonnade—Mt. Clemens
Mark—helo crash—drugs (?)—Detroit—
Toni—elections—Chase/Mt. Clemens
Tanaka—D.C.—past history

He drew lines between the related items. A picture was vaguely forming in his head, but it still wasn't coming together. He needed to talk to Mark and Beverly. In fact, he thought, it might not be a bad idea to have dinner with Karen after all. Perhaps she could fill in additional information on the election, and why it would attract the attention of someone like Tanaka. The phone rang.

Dexter grabbed the receiver. "Dexter Racine."

The phone crackled, then Mark's voice came in clearly. "So you found her?"

"Yes. Her name is Toni Daniels. I think you are off target on her involvement in your crash, though. She's a political finance consultant. As a matter of fact, she works for Michigan's former Lt. Governor—who's a shoo-in for next governor. I doubt she's involved with drugs."

"I don't know about any elections, but I have Caterina here with me. She just came from—Toni is it? Toni's cottage where she killed a hired assassin, one of *Toni's* men. And we just had a shoot out with a few more guns. Caterina says she works for some organization called Tierrasante. Check that company out, I understand they are based stateside. We're coming in, Dex. It's getting too hot down here."

Dexter felt a chill run up his spine. Did Mark say Caterina killed an assassin? He had heard *Tierrasante* before. He looked at the notes he'd scribbled. Beverly was working with that company. And they sponsored the real estate project, Mt. Clemens. The pieces were starting to make a picture. And Dexter didn't like the picture it was making.

"This is more serious than I thought, Mark. Beverly might be involved in this somehow as well."

Mark was incredulous. "Are you kidding? What would Beverly be doing involved with Brazil or Detroit?"

"When I spoke to her last, just before I came down to find you, she mentioned she was working on a housing project in Philly for a company named—get this—Tierrasante. Tierrasante is also the sponsor of a land project here in Detroit. A land project that is sponsored by Lt. Governor Chase, Toni Daniel's employer. And—it was just approved by the governor—which, the buzz is, will ensure the election of Chase as the next governor of Michigan."

"Listen, We're coming in, Dex. We'll try and get a flight out of São Paulo this afternoon. That should bring us into Detroit sometime tomorrow morning. I'll bring the other items with me."

Dexter gripped the phone. "Be careful man. This looks like it's turning into something very big and very ugly. I'm trying to get a hold of Bev now, see what she knows."

There was a pause on the line, and then Mark said more quietly, "Make sure she's safe, Dex. Don't let anything happen to our girl."

Caterina noticed Mark's concern as he mentioned this unknown "our girl." She suspected she heard more than she wanted to know.

Dexter's voice was grave as he answered, "You know I won't man. You know I won't. I'll check the flights and meet you at the airport tomorrow morning."

Dexter hung up the phone and tried to reach Beverly again. She was not in the office yet, nor had she checked her messages. Dexter left a message on her home machine as well and then hung up. Where the hell was she?

Chapter 36

Young stormed into Edward's suite. "Out. Everyone. *Now.*"

Chang was on the phone. He hung up quickly and stood, watching his bodyguards and staff beat a hasty retreat. Willing himself to remain cool, he walked to the bar and took out two glasses. "Can I get you something, Greg?"

"Glenlivet. Two fingers on the rocks. Where is Toni?" Young sat on the sofa and took the glass Edward handed him.

Chang sat on the chair opposite the couch. "She's meeting with Tanaka and his party now, as you requested."

"Damn it, Edward. This grand scheme of yours is turning into a real mess. I want this Mark taken care of. Immediately. I don't want to hear any excuses and no more mistakes. This could cost *you* big. Do I make myself clear?"

Edward gulped his drink down and put it on the coffee table. "Sir, I have every assurance that Mark Davis will not be a problem for us. I am waiting now for a final report on—" The phone rang.

Edward glanced at Young, who waved his hand impatiently. "Get it. It might be good news."

Chang picked up the phone. "Yeah."

Young watched as Chang's face blanched. His mouth twitched as he listened to the person talking. Slowly, he replaced the receiver, and then turned to Young, his eyes fearful.

"That was Brazil. There was a shoot out. Several of our men were taken out. Mark Davis and Caterina Quebas got away."

Young threw his glass across the room and stood, face red, trembling with anger. "Tanaka must not hear about this. Call the investors and change our meeting to breakfast. I want the mess in Brazil cleaned up before anyone else hears about it. Then we are going to sit down and you are going to work out a plan that convinces me that I shouldn't slit your throat and dump your idiot body in the lake."

Young stalked over to the phone and dialed Beverly's room number. No answer. He slammed the phone down and stomped over to the suite door, swinging it open. "Where is the Madsen woman?"

The bodyguard spoke quickly and quietly into his receiver, then turned back to Young. "Sir, she was seen going down to the hotel coffee shop with Mr. Towers about fifteen minutes ago. Do you want me to send someone down for her?"

Young took a deep breath and straightened his tie. In a voice almost restored to its usual tenor, he said, "No. That's fine. I'll go down myself."

Young turned back to glare at Chang. "I'll be back shortly to finish dealing with you."

When the door finally slammed behind Young, Chang's muscles melted and he slumped into his chair.

Chapter 37

The three men stood, as Toni approached them, and waited until she was settled in her seat before they resumed theirs. Toni motioned for a waiter "Please have them serve now." She turned to the men.

"We are so honored to have you here in Detroit, Mr. Tanaka. I hope your accommodations are comfortable?"

'Very suitable, thank you. Ms. Daniels, I would like to introduce Mr. Epstein and Mr. Carey."

Toni nodded her head at them. "Gentlemen, good to finally meet you." Turning back to Tanaka, she said, "I'm afraid this meeting will have to be brief, sir. There are some minor complications that need attending to before the convention, I am sure you understand. However—" Toni stopped as two waiters came over to the table carrying a platter of live fish sliced open. Toni smiled, "In honor of your visit, Mr. Tanaka."

Tanaka's face smoothed with pleasure as the platter was placed on the table. Mr. Epstein's face blanched as he watched the gills and eyes move on the fish Mr. Tanaka was even then, digging into.

Tanaka closed his eyes and savored the first bite. "Superb, gentlemen please enjoy" He turned to Toni. "Your attention to detail does not go unnoticed, Ms. Daniels. Now, let us get to the business at hand."

Toni pulled a folder from her briefcase and opened it on the table. She looked up at Mr. Carey. "Mr. Carey, I believe, does not feel that the Port of Baltimore is receiving the promised revenue percentages in the third quarter. While Jacksonville traffic has almost doubled in the past year, the unions have been stifling the loading of traffic at Baltimore."

Mr. Tanaka dabbed his mouth gingerly and placed the napkin back in his lap. "Perhaps we should consider closing…"

Mr. Carey interrupted. "That is not acceptable—uh…with all due respect sir, my family has worked hard to build the Port."

Tanaka rubbed his chin thoughtfully, "I am sure we can find a solution, Mr. Carey, but we are limited in our ability to assist just now."

Toni interrupted, "Gentlemen, I have been authorized by Mr. Chang to present the following numbers regarding The Colonnade Project. I think these projections will solve each of our individual and collective problems in one fell swoop. I'd like to direct your attention to this chart. We have completed eight cities and identified two new centers. Revenues on these projects have exceeded estimates by 34% and Phase I was completed almost two years ahead of schedule. We have been investigating the possibility of moving the Baltimore project up from a Phase III to II, thereby increasing revenues in that sector by 23% by year two and 47% by completion date."

Toni handed out copies of the charts and there was a murmur of assent, as the men more closely scrutinized the numbers. Toni smiled inwardly. Getting Tanaka behind them on this project was sure to gain her and Edward's entry into the executive washrooms of Tierrasante.

It had been Toni's idea to bump the Baltimore deal up. She was certain that such a move would nip in the bud an internal fight between Carey's group, who didn't want to relinquish control of that water port, and Tanaka's interests, who couldn't afford the kind of public, gangland war

Carey's people were prepared to wage. That meant Tanaka et al owed Edward and her for bringing in this mutually advantageous solution.

But bringing Tanaka the next Michigan governor to add to his toy chest of political minions was the *piece de resistance*. It was the beginning of a whole new game. As they moved to ensnare politicos in the Tierrasante web, Toni intended that she and Edward would be positioned at the very apex of that web. Toni almost smacked her lips in anticipation.

The noise levels in the restaurant suddenly rose dramatically, shaking Toni out of her Reverie. She shrank back into booth, as she spotted the Mayor making his way into the crowded bar, followed by a series of photographers.

Toni turned calmly to Mr. Tanaka. "Sir, as you are aware, I am working for Lt. Governor Chase' campaign, the details of the short and long term benefits of that alliance is detailed in this report. I cannot, however, be—" Toni's attention was again distracted by a handsome black man's face in the crowd. It looked vaguely familiar to her but she couldn't place the face. She shook her head to clear it and turned back to the matter at hand.

"As I was saying, Mr. Tanaka, I am certain you'll understand that I need to leave this meeting in as circumspect a manner as possible. This is not the environment for a Chase supporter just now."

Mr. Tanaka stood, "Of course, Ms. Daniels. I will look over the details of your report and we will talk again this evening, ok?"

Toni shook Tanaka's hand. "Thank you sir." She stood, as did the gentlemen. "I hope we will have opportunity to talk at greater length, Mr. Carey, Mr. Epstein. It is—" Suddenly, Toni recalled where she'd seen that handsome man's face. At the airport in Ilhéus, just after she saw Mark—it was too much coincidence. She had to get in touch with Edward.

Gathering up her briefcase, Toni said, "I'm terribly sorry about the abrupt departure, but...I must get back." With that, Toni jumped up from the table and raced out of the back door of the restaurant.

Once she found herself in the alleyway, she took her phone out and dialed Edward's number. It rang three times. Toni was about to hang up, when he answered.

"Edward, it's Toni. Things are getting complicated. I just saw a man I ran into at the airport in Ilhéus. A black man, Edward and only a few minutes after I saw—yes, I know I saw him—Mark. Oh god, Edward, they've followed me back here. That means they have the bag."

Chang's voice was deadly calm. "What bag is that, Toni?"

The iciness in Edward's voice chilled, but also calmed Toni. This was not the place—and Edward Chang was not the person—for her to fall apart. Her voice was steady again when she replied, "The bag Larry gave me to take care of Jorge, Edward. The bag with my international license, the helo schematics, maps—hell, even a back up disk of some of my memos to you. I was certain it had all gone up in the crash, certainly, we combed the area and found nothing, I swear."

"And Tanaka?"

"I just left him happily digging into a platter of live fish. He is very pleased with the numbers on the Baltimore proposal. I know that bringing Chase' in is going to be the key, Edward. I'm going to make a call down to Larry and get a status report. We have to get a hold of that pilot and the bag. Now, I'm fairly certain he hasn't passed the information over to anyone yet, because the disk is encoded. His friend didn't recognize me when I walked by him. I think we are all right, but I'll make the connection south and call back with confirmation. Edward, we just need a little more time. The primaries are less than 72 hours away. Chase will be the new governor and we'll be home free. But we have to get that bag."

Chang's voice was quiet. "You told me this was contained, Toni. Get your ass up here. *Now.* I want to know what's going on." He slammed down the phone.

Toni ended the call and reached for a cigarette, then cursed. She hadn't smoked in three months, but she really needed one now.

She had to get that bag. She was no fool. If that bag wound up in the wrong hands, Toni wouldn't live to hear about it. And it wouldn't matter one whit that she and Edward had been partners and lovers for years, when he looked her in the eye and pulled the trigger. He would do it himself too. He'd want to tell her how much she'd disappointed him, before he killed her.

Well, she thought, *Edward's wrath can be just as easily assuaged.* She simply had to find the pilot. She tapped her finger on her chin. She would find the pilot where she found that alley cat, that Caterina, no doubt. Checking her watch, Toni did a quick time calculation. By now, Caterina should have been eliminated, and Larry would be preparing to leave for Cuba. She might catch him at his apartment packing. She dialed the number and waited impatiently as it rang three times, four, five. No answer.

She disconnected and dialed the cottage and then Larry's cell phone. *No answer.* She was getting concerned. Larry always had his phone with him. He had *orders* to keep it near him. And there was no answer at the cottage either? Toni's heart was racing as she dialed the Estate. After giving the pass codes, she was connected to the office.

As she listened to the Estate manager's report, Toni felt herself go limp. The phone slipped from her fingers and crashed to the concrete at her feet. *It was too late. She was a dead woman.*

Chapter 38

Beverly stirred sugar into her coffee cup. "Well, Stan, you look much better than you did earlier this evening. I don't know why I really worried, you always pull through."

Stan grinned. "Yeah, well, I had to get a few things in order, which I have. Now I am ready to focus on our success and getting rich. Are you?"

Beverly laughed. "Am I? With the package Greg has put together for me, I am going to have the life of my fantasies."

Stan looked down at his mug for a moment, and then continued. "That's great, Bev. I knew they'd make it worth your while. But remember what I told you before; with all this money comes a lot of hours and a lot of work. Have you talked to your fiancé about it yet?"

Beverly frowned. "No. I haven't."

Stan smiled wryly. "Is that macho man of yours still on his mission? You know, this is a big move and we are going to be moving really fast. Maybe you can get in touch with him, you know, have that talk. Once you sign on, they aren't going to want to hear about your man wanting you home to cook dinner." Stan tried to laugh. "Where is he anyway?"

Beverly looked away for a moment and fought back tears. She turned back to Stan, her voice steady as she answered, "This has happened very fast, but I won't have a problem with Mark, so don't concern yourself with that. I am in. I'll deal with juggling my personal life on my time. Okay?"

"Okay, sure. No problem. We're a team, so I worry. With your wedding coming up, Mark being out of town, this new opportunity…I know it's a lot to handle—and he's been away for a while, that's all. Where did you say he was?"

Beverly pushed her coffee aside and leaned in to Stan, her voice firm and unbending. "I didn't, Stan. And frankly, I don't want to discuss the matter any further. I appreciate your concern, but enough. Okay? Just know that I'm in and will be available to do the work I need to do, as always. Now, can we change the subject? We have a meeting in half an hour."

Stan shrugged and then smiled. "Sorry. I didn't mean to pry. Why don't we go over the investor profiles one more time?"

Beverly sighed in relief, the tension in her shoulders dissipating. "Thank you, Stan. I'm going to run to the powder room and freshen up now, so we can work right up until it's time to go in to the meeting."

"I'll get us fresh coffee." As Stan watched Beverly walk away, he saw Young scanning the crowd. Young saw him too, and made his way over to their table.

He sat opposite Stan. "Do you have my information, Mr. Towers?"

Stan ducked Young's intense glare and looked down at his cup. "I'm afraid I wasn't able to get the information you needed, Mr. Young. I can only push her so far, without her getting suspicious. She doesn't want to talk about Mark. At least, not to me. I think you'd better work out another way to get those details, sir. I'm sorry."

Young answered briefly, "I'm sorry too, Stan."

"Well, Greg. How nice of you to join us. We were just doing some last minute prep for the meeting."

Young stood up and took Beverly's hand. "Please, sit. I am afraid some business has come up that requires my immediate attention. The investors meeting had to be rescheduled. We'll meet with them over breakfast tomorrow morning, eight o'clock. I know you have flights out at twelve, and I don't want to keep you here longer than necessary. I can see you have everything in readiness. It is very refreshing to have such diligent professionals on our team.

"Why don't you meet me in my suite at seven, tomorrow morning so we can discuss that package we've put together for you. I hope you found it acceptable. Now, if you'll excuse me, I must return to the suite and return calls."

He bowed slightly. "Ms. Madsen, Mr. Towers." Young turned and walked out.

Stan snorted derisively. "Isn't he just too slick? 'I hope you found it acceptable.'"

Beverly stood. "I really don't know what's been bugging you lately, Stan, but you'd better pull it together. I'm glad the meeting is postponed. It's been a long day and tomorrow is going to be even longer. I'm going to bed—and I suggest you do the same. Maybe a good night's sleep will get you back on course."

Stan sat back in his chair, his face sullen. Beverly's tone softened, "I'll be up for a while reading. Call me if you want to talk, okay? I'm really worried about you, Stan. Will you call me if you want to talk?"

Stan nodded his head. "Thanks Bev. You're the best. But I'll be alright. This is one problem I am going to have to handle myself."

Chapter 39

"Why don't we grab lunch before we go back to the office. I must admit, I am not looking forward to giving Emmanuel my letter of resignation."

Beverly and Stan were driving away from the airport. The skyline of Philadelphia loomed on the horizon.

Stan glanced over at Beverly with a sly grin. "You'll get over it. Just as soon as you see that first ten percent come in...or maybe when you hand over the down payment on your new palace?"

"Stop it. I'm really nervous about it. I mean, I'm excited too. The meeting this morning with Greg was wonderful. There's nothing like someone wanting you so much that they roll out the red carpet for you."

Stan laughed. "That's no big deal. All my women roll the red carpet out for Stan the Man. You'll get used to it."

Beverly laughed too. "I don't know why I even talk to you."

"Because you know that deep down, I'm a really nice guy."

"Ha! I know nothing of the sort. You are a cad and a devil all the way to the bone."

Stan looked over at her again, his smile softer. "Well, what if this devil treats to you to a champagne lunch? I really want to celebrate. I'm glad you are on board, Bev. It wouldn't have been nearly as much fun without you."

They drove the rest of the way to the restaurant in companionable silence. They ordered lunch and a talked easily for a while, and then Stan saw a friend walk in.

"Bev, do you mind? I can't believe Don just walked in here. I haven't seen him since undergrad days. I'm just going to run over and say hello."

"Have fun."

Stan chuckled as he stood. "You do that and I'll be right back."

While Beverly waited for Stan to return, she called in to the office. Robin was bursting. "You got an *urgent* call from Dexter Racine. He's in Detroit and you are to call him *immediately.* I can connect the call for you, if you'd like."

Beverly realized that she was slightly tipsy when she said, "I've waited two days for that call...now I think *Mr. Racine* can just wait a few minutes for me."

Robin always wanted to be in the midst of some intrigue. "But Bev, you said to call you wherever you were, you had to talk to him"

Beverly poured the last of the bottle into her glass. "I know I did, and you've been just great looking out for me, Robin. I owe you. But I'm on my way back to the office. I'll call him when I get there. Now, is there anything else?"

She could hear Robin sigh with disappointment. "Yes. Mr. Garrison wants to see you when you get in and you got flowers. A huge bouquet, from..." Beverly could hear Robin opening her card, "Michael and Doris."

"Thank you Robin. Will you have someone deliver them to my desk? I'll see you shortly." She disconnected the call as she saw Stan make his way back to her.

Stan looked refreshed and together as he wove his way briskly over to the table. He stopped in front of Beverly and bowed slightly. With a wry grin, he said "I hope m'lady wasn't kept waiting too long? I've taken care of the bill. Shall we go?"

He held Beverly's chair and, with brows lifted in concern, she stood. "Uh, thank you."

Stan noted Beverly's frown and smiled wider, "I am merely giving you the red carpet treatment you so richly deserve. I will now chauffeur you back to the office and carry you to your desk, lest your shoes get dust upon them."

Beverly, relieved to see the old Stan back, burst into laughter. She poked her finger in to his chest and said, "You, sir, are an idiot!"

"Maybe so, ma'am. Maybe so. I care not to argue with a lady." Laughing, they left the restaurant.

While they waited for the valet to bring the car around, Stan took Beverly's hand, his face somber. "I have to tell you something, Bev, all jokes aside."

The traces of laughter left Beverly as she looked up into Stan's face. "Yes?"

Stan's ears were burning bright red, as he started. "I want you to know that I've always admired you. The way you work, think—who you are."

Beverly started to interrupt, but Stan rushed on. "I am not trying to hit on you again, we've put that behind us, right? We're friends. I just want you to know you mean a lot to me."

Beverly looked away, embarrassed. "I don't know what to say Stan."

Stan put his finger beneath Beverly's chin and lifted her face until she was looking up at him again. "Say that you'll be happy. That you won't let all the money about to come into your life change you or make you compromise who you are. Say that you know that you can always count on me to be in your corner. Alright?"

Beverly studied the sincerity in Stan's face. She nodded. "I know that, Stan."

The car pulled up in front of them, breaking the moment. Stan nodded briskly, "Good. Then take this too." Stan handed Beverly his business card.

"Thank you my good man." He handed the valet a bill and stood back as Beverly climbed in the passenger side.

Shutting the door, Stan went around to the driver's side and tossed his briefcase into the back seat before climbing in behind the wheel. He turned on the radio and pulled away from the curb.

Beverly looked at the back of the card. There was a series of numbers written in pencil on it. "What is this?" Beverly turned to Stan.

"It is the combination to my office safe. You're right Bev. We are partners and friends. I have important documents I keep there and, well, if anything ever happened to me, I wouldn't want just anyone going through them. So will you memorize the numbers and toss that card? It would mean a lot to me."

They drove down Walnut Street in silence. Beverly pondering Stan's strangeness, his comments about the future. The light turned red as they approached the corner, and Stan slowed the car to a stop. Two teenagers approached the line of idling autos, offering to wash windshields for a dollar. As one approached Stan's car, he turned on the windshield wipers and waved the man away impatiently.

"Dirt bags," he muttered. "Those bums don't deserve to live."

Beverly gave Stan a surprised look "Give them a break Stan, they're just trying to make a living."

A well-dressed young man, carrying a legal bag, walked past the front bumper and then looked into the car. He smiled and waved in recognition as he caught Stan's eye and came around to the driver's side window. Stan smiled cautiously and rolled it down a few inches.

"You're Stan Towers, right? Of Canterbury Enterprises?"

"Why yes, yes I am. Do I know you?"

The man shifted his bag to his other hand and reached into the car to shake Stan's hand. "Mr. Towers, I was just heading to your office. I'm from Peabody-Johnson Properties. I was delivering some papers to you."

Stan relaxed. "Ahh, OK. I wasn't expecting anything from Peabody but why don't you let me pull over, so I can take them now. Save you a few minutes."

The man smiled as he stepped back from the car and followed as Stan pulled over to the curb, letting the engine idle. The squeegee men lounged behind the car, waving to oncoming cars for work. Stan ignored them as he rolled his window all the way down, and looked up with a smile as the young man hoisted the bag up on the window and reached in. Pulling out some papers, the man slipped out a pistol fitted with a silencer. As he handed Stan the papers, he shoved the gun into Stan's gut and pulled the trigger twice.

Blood erupted from Stan's chest and he slumped over. Beverly screamed, panicked and grabbed the steering wheel, pushing Stan's leg aside as she stepped on the gas. Startled pedestrians screamed as they jumped away from the curb.

The car careened away from the curb and then crashed into a light post. Stan's head collapsed against the horn and people ran over to the smoking car. The trigger man quickly shoved the gun in his pants and disappeared into the crowd. Out of the crowd, A slim man appeared and ran towards the car shouting, "Somebody call an ambulance!"

He rushed over to the passenger side of the car and opened the door. Beverly sat strapped into the seat, her eyes closed.

A woman ran up behind the slim man and asked, "Is she dead?"

He looked over his shoulder at the woman. "I don't think so, go call an ambulance—there's a phone over there!"

When the woman departed, he knelt down beside Beverly and whispered, "Beverly, Beverly...are you alright? Can you hear me?"

Beverly's vision was blurred as she fought away unconsciousness. As it cleared, she began to make out a man's face, the cold, light blue eyes, but was still too dazed to move. It was Edward Chang. She saw the gun hidden from public view by the his jacket.

Chang whispered, "Beverly...Where is Mark? Beverly—I must know where to find Mark."

Just then, a heavy hand was placed on Chang's shoulder. He tensed as he turned around, looking up into the face of a police officer.

"How is she?"

Chang looked again at Beverly and then, masking his face in mock-concern, closed his jacket and stood, turning to the officer. "I think she's alright, but the man looks dead."

The officer politely pushed him aside and stooped to look into the car. Chang saw several police cars pulling up and could hear the distant whine of an ambulance. He stepped slowly away from the car and melted into the crowd of onlookers.

The patrolman helped Beverly from the car and over to the curb. Beverly looked up and saw Chang's blue eyes in front of a store across the street. He pushed his jacket aside, flashing the butt of his gun at her and then faded away as Beverly fainted.

Chapter 40

Dexter went down to the lobby. The place was a mob scene as conventioneers started pouring in. He pushed his way to the front desk and caught the attention of the concierge. "Just a moment," he called out to the harried man.

The concierge came over to him, a plastic smile plastered on his weary face. He'd been hearing "just a moment" for over seven hours. All he wanted to hear now was the clock toll the hour and signal his shift change. He glanced at the clock. Two more minutes. With a sigh, the man asked blandly, "And how may I assist you sir?"

Dexter took no notice of the man's insincere smile or weariness. "I am looking for Karen Taylor. She's working with—"

The concierge interrupted him. One minute and forty seconds. "Ms. Taylor just went up to the Simmons' hospitality suite to take care of last minute details on the cocktail party. That's room 1639, sir. Will there be anything else I can help you with?"

"No, thank you." Dexter raced off towards the elevator banks.

The concierge looked at the clock. Who was going to care if he ducked out thirty seconds early?

• • •

Toni stared at the phone laying at her feet. *Get a grip*, she admonished herself. She bent down and quickly scooped up the phone. Straightening her suit and patting her hair, she took a deep breath and went back into the hotel.

Alright, so Larry had been found dead at the cottage. Two of her best men had been shot down at Caterina's hotel. Her father was gone. So was she. The manager was sent to clean up to the cottage, so no body, no papers would be found, but neither had his men found the envelope containing the cash, ticket and instructions for Cuba.

There was no sign of Caterina or Mark. The hanger at Ilhéus had been blown up and the roads were being watched, all backup security systems had been put in place, but Toni still had an ominous feeling. What had been put in motion would not so easily be stopped. The question was only, when it would all go down. If she were lucky, there might be enough time to figure out some way to jump clear of the wreckage. Edward already knew about Ilhéus, so she had to steer clear of him until she could figure out things to do. What would she do?

She walked distractedly through the lobby towards the elevator banks. She yelped in surprise and instinctively jerked away, when someone grabbed her arm.

"Hey! Calm down." David Biggs, Chase' personal assistant, blanched in surprise at Toni's response. "Boy are you jumpy! Where have you been? Chase' has had us comb this hotel top to bottom looking for you. He needs to see you urgently."

"Wha—oh, please. I can't meet with him right now, David. Tell him I'll talk to him later." She waved a dismissive hand as she tried to brush past him, but David hooked his arm through Toni's and propelled her on to the elevator.

"Huh uh. This messenger has no intention of being shot. He wants to see you now."

• • •

Toni gathered herself together as she was ushered into Chase' suite. The place was in a flurry. People were rushing about with stacks of paper and banners, the phones were ringing and there was the roar of several voices competing with each other in increasing decibels.

Chase was on the phone, his face flushed with irritation. "This is my campaign, Eric. I don't give a damn what the Free Press has to say. I don't want District 12. Let Simmons have it.... I know it's a large district, but look at the stats. They turn out less than 10% every election. They don't vote. Let Simmons have them. Alright, what about the kid—this Morgan kid? He made the All-American basketball team and was second round draft by Duke. He's bright and clean cut. They'll listen to anything he says. Get him over here. Maybe he can pull us a few votes. What? Eric, the kid probably doesn't give a damn about politics.…What I want is. . " he turned and saw Toni walking towards him.

"Gotta go, Eric. Get a hold of that boy and get back to me tomorrow on that. I want him on stage with me. And do me a favor. Give that beautiful bride of yours a kiss for me. Yeah…you know where! Right. We'll talk later." Chase hung up the phone and went over to Toni, his voice booming jovially.

"Welcome home. We've missed you. Look at this place—it's a mad-house. A lot has happened since you left on your little trip."

Toni noted the false jocularity in Chase' voice and knew something was up. Toni played along, smiling brightly. "So I've been reading. That's why I got back here. Don't want to miss all the fun!"

Chase put his arm around Toni's shoulder and said to the room, "That, gentlemen—and ladies, is why she is the best consultant in the State. You should take notes, Arnie, take my calls too. We'll be in the study. I don't want to be interrupted."

Once the door was closed behind them, Chase' smile was quickly replaced with an irritated scowl. "We've got a problem that needs to be dealt with immediately."

Chase motioned for Toni to have a seat in one of the high-backed leather club chairs. He went to the bar and removed the stopper from the scotch decanter. "Drink? I think you should have one. With or without soda is your choice, but the drink I recommend strongly."

Toni was only half listening, engrossed in her own, more immediate problems. "Fine. Give it to me on the rocks—two fingers. What's the problem?"

Chase handed Toni her drink and settled into the matching chair beside her, swirling his drink around the glass thoughtfully, then swallowing it all down, hard.

"You heard about Mt. Clemens, right? The governor made the announcement earlier this afternoon, as promised."

Chase leaned forward, "What we had hoped, was that the timing would boost my points in the polls—but it has done far more than that, Toni. We couldn't have anticipated the run in between the governor and Simmons. We couldn't have paid for a better performance for the press. The fall out? The Governor has been discredited because he stupidly announced it at the same time he announced school budget cuts, while at the same time, the jobs and income to the state are undeniable. That alone has delivered a large segment of your community into our camp and ushered me right into the governor's mansion."

Toni chose to ignore the 'your community' comment. Instead, she too sat forward, a mask of enthusiasm firmly in place. "That's wonderful, Dick. So? What's the problem?"

Chase put his glass on the floor beside the chair and stood. "Chang. He's pressing me. I thought he'd wait until after the elections to make a move—when I was in a better and less public position to deal with him. Well, all the projections have me in office already, he is trying to cozy up *now*. I am not about to have that hoodlum in any kind of continued close association with me—particularly when victory is so close. My position is, he got his land deal and I got the governor's seat. If he had left it at that, everything would have been fine. But he hasn't.

"So we have to figure out how to keep Mt. Clemens alive—at least until after the convention—while getting that psycho off my back and out of my picture. Permanently is preferred, but until after the election will do. And we have to act quickly—the convention starts tomorrow and I want nothing in my way. Ideas?"

Toni tossed her drink back. Chase wanted to cut Edward out. She smiled slightly. She knew this would happen. The timing of this piece of news was the break she needed. There was no way Edward would allow Chase to walk away, and Chase, arrogant fool that he was, seriously underestimated the danger that was Edward Chang—particularly if he thought Edward could just "be taken care of." She looked up at Chase, her face etched in somber concern.

"Let me ponder the possibilities, Dick. I have a few ideas working here already. We will have to move quickly. Have someone locate Chang for me, but don't make contact. Leave that to me. And you," Toni stood and pushed Chase towards the doors, "get back to work. I'm sure I can come up with an answer to our problem."

Chase smiled and put his hand on Toni's shoulder. "As always, I can count on you. I'll get someone on that. Take as much time as you need." Chase walked over to the doors and then turned back, "but not too much time. The convention is less than twelve hours away. This needs to be done before then."

Chase opened the doors and the noise spilled into the chamber for a moment. When the doors closed behind him, silence was restored. Toni got up and poured another drink.

If she played her cards right, she might just end up on top after all. If she could get them going after each other, she could create a window just big enough to slip through before it all came tumbling down.

Chapter 41

The police officer helped Beverly over to the patrol car. Her head fell back against the vinyl cushion and she struggled to focus. The image of those cold blue eyes, the gun in the waist of the assassin's pants, made her heart pound wildly. She sat up abruptly, a wave of nausea washing over her.

"Just relax, ma'am. You were in an accident and bumped your head. The paramedics will be here to look you over in a second." The officer's voice was warm and soothing.

Beverly closed her eyes for a moment and then they flew open. The man was in the crowd, she'd seen him staring at her. The man who had killed Stan—and had threatened her. She shuddered as she thought about what he might have done had the officer not come up to them when he did.

He asked about Mark. The killer had asked her where he could find Mark. Beverly wrapped her arms around herself and shivered. What was going on? All she knew was that she had to get away. From this crowd, from that man. She didn't know where Mark was—but Dexter did. Yes. She had to get to Dexter.

The policeman was still standing by her, a worried frown creasing his face. She looked up at him and asked weakly, "Do you think you could get me a cup of water or something?"

The officer nodded quickly. "Of course, Ma'am. You just stay put. I'll be right back. After the medics take a look at you, and give you the thumbs up, I have to ask you a few questions, alright?"

Beverly closed her eyes and nodded. "Of course, thank you."

The officer walked quickly away. Beverly peeked through her half-lidded eyes until he disappeared into the throng of people crowding the street. Then she got up, fighting the dizziness that enveloped her, slipped away from the car, and around the corner. She leaned against the wall for a moment, catching her breath, and then staggered over to the curb and hailed a cab.

• • •

Dexter went up to the Simmons' hospitality suite in search of Karen, and answers. It was obvious that an event was about to start. Caterers ran about with buckets of ice, platters of food, table clothes and cutlery. He spotted Karen at the front of the suite, talking to two workers and pointing to the overhead lights.

As he started for her, she moved to the dais that had been set up and began a sound check. "One-two, one-two, Steve, bring this one up a little. One—oh! Hello there!" Karen stepped away from the dais and came over to Dexter, smiling widely.

"I thought I'd seen the last of you, the way you disappeared downstairs. Are you sure you're not a reporter?"

Dexter returned her smile. "I am many things, madam, but a reporter is not one of them…that is, unless you want me to be."

Karen shook her head. "Hmmm. I wish I had time to play with you, handsome, but we have this cocktail party going up shortly. In light of that news flash earlier, this is going to be particularly important. I have to finish preparations, get myself dressed and back here in time to meet and greet…so, will you be here this evening?"

"I think I might just stop by."

"Well good. The event is over at eight, maybe you can make good that dinner offer?"

"I am a man of my word. It would be a pleasure. I'll let you get back to your duties, and I'll see you a little later." He left the suite.

The cocktail party might give him an opportunity to learn more about what was going on with Mt. Clemens and dinner with Karen would fill in the blanks on Chase. He had just enough time to get a shave and fresh suit. But first, he needed to call Beverly's office, again.

• • •

Dexter went back to his room and dialed Beverly's office. The receptionist's voice sounded strained as she answered, "How may I direct your call?"

"Beverly Madsen, please. This is Dexter Racine calling again."

Robin sniffed, "Oh, Mr. Racine, she didn't call you back yet? No. No I guess she didn't have the chance. They were...Mr. Towers and Ms. Madsen were...please hold!"

Dexter looked at the receiver in surprise. *What was going on over there?* A second later, the line opened. This time, a man's voice answered.

"Detective Mike Ferragamo, who am I speaking with?"

"What's going on there? I asked to speak with Ms. Madsen. Is she there? Has something happened?"

Detective Ferragamo's voice barked low and gravelly over the line. "Sir, may I have your name and ask what this call is regarding?"

Dexter knew how to cut to the chase. In his most official Secret Service voice, he said. "My name is Dexter Racine, US Secret Service, Detroit Field Office. Now what's going on?"

"Oh. I'm sorry Agent Racine, Ms. Madsen was involved in a car accident. Now, she's alright, we think. It was reported that Ms. Madsen was a little banged up when she was examined on the scene by the duty officer, but her associate, Stan Towers was killed—shot twice in the chest at close range."

Dexter couldn't believe what he was hearing. Car accident? Shootings? "Where is Ms. Madsen now?"

There was a pause and then the detective answered, "That's what we are trying to discover, Mr. Racine. Ms. Madsen has disappeared."

• • •

Beverly fumbled with her keys and cursed under her breath as she turned it in the lock. Letting herself into her apartment, she pushed the door behind her and rushed into the bedroom. Frantically throwing clothes into an overnight bag, Beverly stumbled out of the bedroom and made her way to the kitchen.

She reached behind the spice rack and withdrew an envelope of cash. Stuffing it into her bag, she picked up the car keys and raced for the front door. Just as she reached out for the door handle, a handkerchief was placed over her nose and mouth. The chloroform it was soaked with burned her eyes and nose, and just before everything went black, she heard the same voice that had whispered to her in the car say, "And where were you going, *girlfriend?*"

Dexter hung up the phone in disbelief. Beverly was missing—maybe hurt. Stan Towers was dead. Dexter mulled over the name for a moment before it came to him. Stan Towers was the man who brought Beverly into Tierrasante. Now he was dead and Beverly was missing.

Dexter paced the floor. Mark and Caterina wouldn't be in until early in the morning and he had to be at the airport to meet them. Was Beverly's disappearance related to this whole Tierrasante mess he was investigating? And if so, would staying in Detroit and unraveling the mystery, lead him to Beverly?

He picked up the phone again and called the front desk. "When does the next flight into Philadelphia leave?"

"The last flight leaves at 7:20p sir. Shall I try and book a seat for you?"

"I'll call you right back." Dexter hung up the phone. What could he accomplish by running around Philadelphia at ten o'clock at night? He sat on the edge of the bed.

Dexter's instincts told him that the answer was here, in Detroit, tied up with this election, with the woman—Toni Daniels, with these land deals and the Tierrasante organization. He went into the bathroom and splashed his face, then went to the closet and took out a fresh shirt. All he could do now, to help any of them, was solve this mystery.

The cocktail party and Karen Taylor was as good a place to start as any.

• • •

When she regained consciousness, Beverly found herself lying on a hard sofa. There was a loud roaring in her ears and her vision was blurred. Her stomach was churning and she thought she was going to be sick. As her vision started to clear, Beverly looked gingerly around.

There was a man seated across from her, strapped into...an airplane seat? Beverly shook her head and tried to focus harder. She realized that she was on a small plane. The roaring she had heard were the engines. They were taking off!

She tried to sit up, but was restrained by a tan, manicured man's hand. "Careful, Beverly, you have a nasty bump on your head."

Beverly turned slowly towards the now familiar voice and looked into the cold blue eyes of Edward Chang. "Who are you? Where are you taking me?"

Chang patted her hand, smiling. "I'm sure you have lots of questions Beverly, and we'll have plenty of time to chat later. You've put us through a lot of trouble, Beverly. I know *my* patience has worn thin. I am giving you one more chance to make this easy on yourself. I suggest you tell me now. Where is Mark Davis?"

• • •

Dexter stood in the doorway of the suite. It was packed with people of all shapes and sizes, all wearing the lurid "Vote Simmons" pin on their lapels.

The jazz band, playing in the front of the room near the dais, was all but drowned out by the laughter and chatter of the throngs of people, getting more raucous as they tossed down the free liquor and stuffed themselves on the myriad appetizers piled high on the tables flanking the walls.

I don't think I'm up for this, Dexter thought. A man came in behind him, shoving Dexter further into the room, as he pushed his way into the crowd, calling out someone's name. Dexter stumbled and fell into a woman. "Excuse me—" he started.

The woman turned around. It was Karen. She had changed into a simple black dress and pearls. Her hair was down and fell in a shiny bob around her shoulders. She smiled and took Dexter's hand. "You don't believe in subtle entrances, do you? And who writes your script? The old 'pardon me, I've stepped on your toe' introduction went out a generation ago."

Dexter laughed with her, taking two glasses of champagne from the passing waiter and handing one to Karen. "Well, I figured you'd probably heard all the good lines, and when in doubt, go with the classics. That's what I always say."

Karen took a sip of her drink and looked over her glass. "Oh, I think you might have a line or two I haven't heard before. As a matter of fact—" She was interrupted by a tap on her shoulder. A gentleman whispered in her ear and then slipped away. She turned back to Dexter.

"We always seem to be interrupted at critical moments. The mayor is ready to speak and it's my job to introduce him. Listen, why don't you meet me down at the restaurant in about half an hour. Have a drink, listen to Simmons—he's got some good ideas. I'll slip out behind you as soon as we're done glad handing. And then—" Karen pulled Dexter's lapel, "we'll finish this conversation to it's logical conclusion." With a wink, she slipped away.

Dexter watched her turn into the professional politico, cool, savvy and well spoken. She primed the audience in well-modulated tones, got them to laugh a bit and then, introduced the mayor to a round of hearty applause.

Simmons stepped up to the dais waving his hands and smiling broadly. He stood proudly while his supporters cheered him, and then settled them down. Dexter backed up to the door of the suite as Simmons began his speech. Karen stood just behind him, scanning the crowd. She caught his eye and discreetly smiled, then turned her attention to Simmons, who had quickly caught his audience up in the passions of the governor's scandal, the budget cutbacks and Mount Clemens.

"This country reeks of corruption, lies, racism…the politics of the privileged! We have always known that, and have fought against it But it is an impossible situation to rectify from outside the walls of power. We must go in to the state house and root out the gluttonous masters. Drive them into the streets to see what their greed has wrought!"

The crowd was going wild. "Yes!"

"That's right, you tell em!"

Simmons quieted them down. "Are you with me? There is no more time to talk that talk, people. We've been talking too long. Chatting about what we need to do; what "they" ought to do—while America is raped right before our eyes. We have to stop talking, because people like Chase will never give the decedents of the Third World the fruit of their blood and labor. No! I say! They are too busy selling America away at our expense, leaving us with the crumbs. We have an obligation to say NO MORE! We have the opportunity to say NO MORE! Tomorrow at the convention, that is what you must say, with your voices, your hearts and your votes—NO MORE CRUMBS! NO MORE CRUMBS!!"

Simmons led his frenzied followers in a chant and as they started clapping their hands and stomping their feet in time with the words, Dexter slipped out the door. *This is where I exit.* He thought. He had his own problems to solve.

He made his way to the restaurant, and after telling the hostess he was expecting a guest, ordering an expresso. Dexter pushed into one of the booths at the back, hidden in the shadows. When the coffee was brought, he sipped it thoughtfully, as he pondered his next moves.

"Young pondered…sloppiness has left us vulnerable to unacceptable risk. There is too much at stake to leave it to Lucien. We've had to take steps here."

A soft, but firm feminine voice answered, "I understand sir. I can leave immediately for Ilhéus, if you wish."

"There is no need. We've made arrangements to have Ilhéus brought to us. Chang is in transit with the woman now. As soon as we have her secured, the Brazil matter will work itself out. How are things with the campaign?"

"Ah, there you are handsome." Karen slid into the booth across from Dexter and motioned for the waitress. "Give me whatever he's drinking. And bring him another one. Thanks." She turned back to Dexter. "Now, where were we?"

Dexter watched as a man slid out of the booth in front of him. A moment later, Toni Daniels slid out as well. She caught his eye and looked startled for a moment, then smiled and head bent towards her companion, they continued talking in low tones as they left the restaurant.

"Don't be fooled by that little red suit, dear. That woman is as cold and hard as a diamond. While I—" Karen took Dexter's hand, "can be a soft and cuddly as a kitten. You do like kittens, don't you?" she purred sexily.

Dexter looked at the beautiful woman sitting across from him, then towards the exit where Toni and her companion had just disappeared. Shaking his head, Dexter turned back to Karen. "Darling, I love kittens."

• • •

Dexter turned on the light and allowed Karen to pass him and enter his suite. Closing the door behind him, he loosened his tie, smiling as he walked over to where Karen now stood, her shoes kicked off near a chair.

"Would you care for a drink?" Dexter offered as he moved smoothly to the bar.

Karen padded behind him, rubbing her hands up his back. "I've had enough to drink," she purred. "Now, I am *very* hungry."

Dexter turned to Karen, two champagne flutes in his hands. With a crooked smile (he thought he'd try the Belafonte move) and his deepest baritone, he said, "I think we should have a toast."

Karen took the glass of golden bubbles and looked up at Dexter with coy, teasing eyes. "What shall we toast to?"

"To possibilities, my dear. Possibilities. To being at the right place at the right time and the fortuitous meeting of two like minds?"

Karen smiled wisely as she clinked Dexter's glass, and watched him watch her take a sip between her red, glossy lips.

She put her drink aside and ran her hands up Dexter's chest. He stood still, watching her unbutton his shirt with a practiced hand, kissing his lightly haired chest as she went.

As his mind wandered with the sensation of Karen's lips and nails grazing him, it stopped short at the images of Beverly and Mark. Beverly, missing, probably unaware of the full danger she was in; and Mark, his maverick brother, even now making his way to the States, after having been ambushed by the mysterious woman Dexter was now tracking down.

And if that weren't enough, there was the possibility that they were both connected to a case he himself had been working on for some time *and* a political race for which such a scandal would have national repercussions.

And here he stood, in his hotel room, about to make love with a beautiful, sensuous woman (who was, just then, beginning to unbuckle his belt) as if he had nothing else to do!

Dexter reached down and pulled Karen to her feet. They kissed passionately and Dexter put his hands into the tangle of her hair, pulling her in for a closer, more probing kiss. For a moment, he was lost in the moment and fantasized that it was Beverly he was kissing.

That sobered him up immediately. He pulled back and held Karen at arms length, her mouth kiss-swollen and lipstick smeared. He smiled apologetically at her heat-filled face and shook his head. "I'm sorry, Karen. You have no idea how very sorry I am, but I can't do this."

Karen's face changed from dreamy passion to irritation. "What do you mean 'can't do this?' Why not?"

Karen sat on the edge of the bed with a frustrated sigh. "If you are worried about what will happen in the morning, let me assure you that I understand Life, my friend. We are two adults, in this place at this time,

in need of a little mutual…comfort. Tomorrow we return to our lives, no
tearful good byes, no talk of the future."

Dexter walked over to Karen and stroked her cheek as he smiled regret-
fully. "If only things were that simple."

Karen looked into Dexter's face and saw that they would not go any
further. "Oh well," she sighed. "Can I at least get that massage?"

• • •

Dexter stared up at the ceiling and watched the dancing streaks of light
that filtered into the room from the city outside. He swung his long legs
off the loveseat he had fallen asleep on and groaned as he stretched his
back. Karen lay sprawled across the bed, snoring lightly. Dexter watched
her for a moment and then pulled the covers over her bare shoulders,
chuckling to himself.

He had felt badly that he had started something with Karen that he
could not complete, and so had given her one of his very best Shiatsu mas-
sages. He felt her tense muscles melt under his strong hands, enjoyed her
moans of decadent pleasure which eventually gave way to the light snore
of satisfied sleep.

Dexter curled his lanky body into the love seat and hoped for a few
hours rest. There was a lot going down in the next few days and Dexter
wanted to be sharp and in top form, but he hadn't been able to do more
than restlessly doze. Quietly moving over to the table by the window,
Dexter tried to make out the position of the hands on his watch. It looked
like it was almost two o'clock.

He considered laying beside Karen on the warm bed for a few more hours,
but decided to get dressed instead. The conversation he'd overheard in the
restaurant was still niggling at the back of his mind. Toni had been discussing
Brazil with a man whose face, Dexter had not seen. *Ilhéus.* It was just too
much of a coincidence. He had to find Toni and there wasn't much time.

He picked up the phone and quietly called the operator. "Any messages
for Dexter Racine?"

"Yes sir, you have two. The first reads: "in from Brazil 8:40," the caller said you'd understand. The second is from a 'Bremmer' who says to return the call urgently. Time no object. He left a number sir. 202-555-5555."

"Got it. Thank you. Have a good evening." Dexter hung up the phone. So Mark and Caterina would be at the airport at 8:40. He hoped Bremmer was calling with information on Toni and the license. He'd have to call from the lobby.

He gathered up his clothes and leaned over to kiss Karen's forehead. She stirred and smiled, but didn't awaken. He jotted a quick note to her and left it on the empty pillow beside her. Then he picked up his briefcase and slipped out.

Beverly's head was pounding, both from the shock of the car accident and the drugs they'd used on her to get her…to wherever she was. She realized that she was probably in shock as well. She wished, futilely, that she could just crawl into her bed and go to sleep. Her exhausted mind whispered to her that if she just went to sleep, this nightmare would end. But each time she felt herself starting to nod off, she would look at the man standing guard at the door, or the one by the window, and their guns, and the heaviness that was stealing up her legs and arms would dissipate again.

Where was Chang? She wondered. *Where am I?* She had no idea where she was or what time, even what day it was. When she had been unable to answer Chang's questions about Mark—he thought she was refusing— he'd given her an injection. She remembered the sensation of floating off into semi-consciousness. There was a cold breeze, she remembered, the roar of…engines? A dark night sky and stars. A lot of stars or, or lights. Being carried to…she didn't know. And then blackness, until now.

She might have believed it was all a dream…the sensation of being on a airplane, or taking off, of the cold blue eyes…of…Stan…But the pounding in her head was real. And she was still wearing the clothes she'd had on earlier, clothes that were splashed with blood—Stan's blood—on her blouse and skirt.

She tried to speak, but her throat was sore and dry. *Where am I?* She screamed in her head, though it came out as a hoarse whisper.

"You are in Detroit, Ms. Madsen. Are you comfortable?" A hand appeared in front of her with a tumbler of ice water. She took the glass hesitantly and looked up as she drank—into the face of—Mr. Young! Behind him stood Chang, his cold blue eyes smiling sardonically at her.

Beverly eyes were filled with horror. "Mr. Young…that…that…killer," she swallowed hard, trying to push the words out

Mr. Young sat beside Beverly and patted her shoulder. "Now, now, let's not call ugly names. Mr. Chang works with me. Edward?" He nodded for Chang to join him.

"You two haven't been properly introduced. This is Beverly Madsen, our newest real estate star. Beverly, Edward heads up operations here in Detroit, I told you about him at our dinner last night. He is the mastermind of the Mount Clemens project, among other things."

Chang stuck his hand out. "A pleasure to meet you. I've heard so much about you, Ms. Madsen."

Beverly stared at the outstretched hand, and then turned back to Mr. Young. "Why have you brought me here? What is it that you want?"

Mr. Young frowned slightly. "Edward, I thought you told the lovely Ms. Madsen our needs." With a sigh, he turned back to Beverly.

"It's really quite simple, Beverly. We need to be in contact with your fiancé. He has some things that belong to us, that we very desperately need back. I'm sorry that we had to go to such extraordinary lengths and involve you, but as I said, it is rather important that we reach him as quickly as possible."

Beverly closed her eyes against Mr. Young's face. She could hardly believe that only hours earlier, she'd been sitting across from this man whom she'd found charming and intriguing, this man who'd seduced her with his offers of power and fortune. She'd had drinks with him, laughed with him—she and Stan had laughed with him. And now Stan was dead and she was being held hostage.

Young placed his hands on either side of Beverly's face. "Beverly. This is not the time for childish games. Look at me."

"I refuse to talk to you so long as that murderer is standing there." She turned her face away again.

"Edward, leave us. I'll call you if I need you." Young watched Chang leave the suite, then turned back to Beverly, his voice was calm, but tinged with irritation. "It is obvious that you don't understand the seriousness of your predicament. You know what this is about. Mark must have talked to you, otherwise you could not have shared his fascinating story with me."

Young stood and started pacing the floor in front of Beverly. "Your fiancé is to blame for all of this. We hold nothing against you."

Beverly glared up at him. "Well, if that's the case, I guess I'll be on my way."

Young clenched his jaw and narrowed his eyes. "Cute Beverly. Why are you protecting him? He is nothing but a courier, a greedy drug courier who thought he could double cross us and leave Brazil with our merchandise. He is a man of no honor, something I'd think you'd abhor.

"He has stolen from us and he has lied to you, leaving you at the altar to run off with another woman. He isn't worth your putting your life in danger. He has proven that he would not do the same for you. He is nothing—but you?

"You are smart, beautiful and talented, Beverly. We need people like you. Honest, loyal people—and although just now, your loyalty is misplaced, I respect it. Really. You can still have an extremely lucrative career with us, Beverly. You could be one of our top executives. Why throw this chance away? We will get Mark, make no mistake about that. So why make this more difficult on yourself than it has to be?"

Beverly flinched inwardly at Young's referral to her and Mark, but her face revealed nothing. "I have told you over and over again, that I have no idea where Mark is. I haven't seen or heard from him in several weeks. But even if I did know, I wouldn't tell you. Whatever is going on between Mark and me, is my affair to deal with. I don't believe Mark ran drugs for you—but I do believe that you are the lowest sort of scum, a pusher in an expensive suit. And as for your generous offer, I wouldn't work with you—or your dirty organization under any circumstance."

Young sat in the chair opposite Beverly. "Don't draw conclusions about something you know nothing about, Ms. Madsen. Tierrasante is legitimate. It is one of the fastest growing commercial and real estate development corporations in America today. Every state in this nation wants us to build the next Village in their backyard.

"And why? Because we are successful, profitable and undeniably the future of this nation. Make no mistake about it, we only give Americans what they want, so don't fool yourself. They don't care where the money comes from. They want the American dream and they don't want it tomorrow—they want it now."

Beverly stared stonily at Young and said nothing. He slammed his hand on the table beside him and stood abruptly. "You know so little, Ms. Madsen. Perhaps that is why you were not able to hold on to your fiancé."

Beverly refused to rise to his bait. She changed the subject. "What did Stan have to do with all of this? He didn't even know Mark."

Young smiled evilly. "Stan Towers. Stan Emerson Towers. Son of a senator, Boston College valedictorian, Wharton MBA. Mr. Towers was bait, Ms. Madsen.

"People like Stan keep the dream alive. They want to live lavish lifestyles, but they don't want to pay the price. They want huge homes, three cars, luxury vacations and the best schools for the kids."

"And is that so wrong to want that?" Beverly asked.

"No, it's not. Except America can no longer afford it. You, of all people, should know that. American's consume over fifty times more than they produce. Someone has to pay for it Beverly, usually the poor. Tierrasante simply provides promising citizens with the means to exercise their right to be in endless debt."

"Financed with drug money," Beverly sneered.

Young smiled, "Finance is a respectable term, Beverly. Yes, we finance the American dream. And we are rewarded with a high yield, for this low risk investment. Our concept isn't unique. We're as mainstream as this..." Young pulled out a platinum credit card and a vial of cocaine. Beverly turned away, disgusted, as Young continued.

"Low risk, long term security. We're betting on greed—and we are heading for the winner's circle. What can you say about a country where the newest and largest mall is a symbol of a town's progress? Americans are willing to pay a very high premium to feel good about themselves. Even if they can't afford it. And my dear, either credit cards or drugs will keep them there."

Young had made his way back over to the sofa and leaned over Beverly, smiling smugly as he held the card and the cocaine in her face. Beverly suddenly swung her clasped hands, slamming Young between the legs. He grimaced and fell to the floor as Beverly ran for the door, banging her leg against the table.

"Grab her," Young grimaced painfully. The man at the door grabbed Beverly and swung her around and against the desk. Blood trickled from her leg as she stood there, arms pinned behind her, watching Young painfully stand and walk over to her.

He looked at her for a moment, and then slapped her hard across the cheek, turning and walking to the window. "I'm sorry you felt you had to do that, Ms. Madsen. I had hoped you would understand the vision, see that we offered you a great future. You cannot stop what is going to happen, Ms. Madsen. Had you been smarter, you would have realized that and made certain that it did not happen to you. It's a pity. Goodbye, Ms. Madsen."

Young limped to the door. As he opened it and stepped into the hallway, he said calmly over his shoulder, "Brad, once the convention is in high gear, take the bitch out to the warehouse and get rid of her." Then he closed the door behind him and was gone.

Chapter 42

Traffic was extremely heavy into and out of the airport. Dexter cursed to himself as his car inched along the highway. He had left the hotel in plenty of time, he thought, to get to the airport before Mark and Caterina's flight came in. He looked at his watch. Their plane would be calling in for clearance about now, which left Dexter about half an hour to get in there.

He pulled up to the airline's terminal with less than ten minutes to spare. No time to look for parking. Hitting the hazard signal, he stepped from the car. An officer came over to him immediately, "I'm sorry sir, this is a no-standing zone. You'll have to move your vehicle."

Dexter reached into his wallet and flashed his badge. "Official business."

The officer stepped back. "I'm sorry sir. Go right through. I'll keep an eye on your car. Will you be long?"

Dexter slammed the door shut and looked at his watch. "I don't think so. Less than half an hour." He came around the car and stepped up to the officer. "Thank you for your assistance," he peered at the officer's badge, "Stocker." I'll remember your cooperation in my report."

He rushed by Stocker into the terminal. Stocker saluted Dexter's back and grinned, "Thank you, sir. We're all in this together!" he shouted after Dexter.

A green Volvo pulled up behind Dexter's car. Stocker stomped over. "Hey bud! Move that car. Can't you see this is a no standing zone?"

• • •

Dexter stood at the gate as the plane deboarded. He recognized Mark's figure towering over the other passengers as he made his way through the passageway into the waiting area. Dexter went over to the door.

"Good to see you, man. Sincerely." He gave Mark a quick hug and hand shake.

Caterina was just behind Mark. She stepped up to Dexter and gave him a weary hug. "*Como vai*? I'm sorry I didn't get to say goodbye to you before you left."

Dexter smiled. "Well, a lot was going on, no?" His face turned serious. "We have to move. Did you check bags?"

"Travel light, travel far, Ace. We have what we wear. Under the circumstances, it wasn't possible to break out the Louie Vuiton. We can pick up a few things when we get to the hotel."

They walked swiftly through the terminal and out to the street.

"Things have gotten really hot since we talked. Do you think you were followed?" Dexter unlocked the car doors and slipped behind the driver's seat.

Mark opened the other door and allowed Caterina to climb in. "I doubt it. If someone was following us, I would have made them by now."

"They have Beverly. They're holding her hostage at the hotel. Everything is set up for surveillance."

Mark turned to Dexter, "Give me your piece."

Dexter pulled away from the curb. As they made their way out of the airport, Dexter reached under his seat and extracted a HK 9mm automatic. "No need, I've brought you your favorite."

Mark took the gun and examined it. "Good looking out, bro. So we're going to break her out in style." Mark's face was grim. "I can hardly wait."

"Well, you're going to have to. We have to get her out without attracting attention."

Caterina asked, "Can't we tell the police there is a hostage in the hotel?"

Dexter shook his head. "Negative. Beverly is wanted for questioning in Philadelphia for the murder of her colleague, Stan Towers. If the police get involved, it will take us forever to find out what's really going on. This is bigger than we thought, Mark. A lot of politicos are involved in this—state and national. You'd be amazed at how easily this case could get stonewalled and Beverly will most certainly be offered up as a sacrifice.

"What I still haven't pieced together, is why Chase would get himself involved in a kidnapping and murder. There are still some things that just don't add up, so we have to be very careful. There is also the democratic convention being held there, so security is tight. We have to figure out a way to get in and out of there quickly and quietly. Once we have Bev safe, I can call in the troops."

Chapter 43

Mark's body was rigid with tension as he paced the room. He turned and sat again, watching Dexter for a moment. Dexter was intently listening through his headset to the movements inside of Young's hotel suite and adjusting the dials on the recording machine beside him.

Mark leaned over and whispered, "What's happening in there?"

Dexter turned a bit and said, "Nothing. It's still quiet. But they're in there, I can hear movement."

Mark slapped his leg impatiently. "We've been sitting here for three hours, already, while she's in there with those…who knows what they've done to her! She could be hurt, hell, she might not even be in there. I say we make our move now."

Caterina came up behind Mark and massaged his neck and shoulders, leaning over to kiss him gently. "And what about this Chase? He must have known about the South American money."

Mark stilled Caterina's hand, then pulled it to his lips and kissed her palm. "Baby, make me a drink, will you?"

Caterina moved to the bar as Dexter removed one of the earphones. "Well, if he didn't, he deserves to get caught—for stupidity. This isn't the first time Ms. Toni has been out of the country. In fact, for the past three years she's been travelling rather frequently. Four times to Colombia, once to Hong Kong and twice to Uruguay and Brazil. He couldn't have—wait!" Dexter adjusted the earphones and leaned in intensely, before throwing the earphones aside. "They're moving!"

Mark moved to the door and put one hand on the knob, one on the frame. He waited a beat and then slowly opened it, holding his breath and hoping it didn't squeak. He caught a glimpse of a woman's skirt and the back of a man as they disappeared into the stairwell. He turned to Dexter and whispered, "Out the back way."

They quickly holstered their guns and, followed the men down the backstairs. As they burst out into the alleyway, guns drawn, Dexter saw their car disappear around the corner.

"What were they driving?" Mark asked as they climbed into the rented Explorer SUV.

"Gray Lexus. Let's go."

They pulled off and followed behind the Lexus at a safe distance, so as not to be detected. Mark reached past Caterina and turned on the radio. When he found a station he wanted, he cranked up the volume and put on his sunglasses.

Caterina looked over at him, a quizzical look on her face. "What are you doing?"

Mark smiled as he screwed a silencer on to the barrel of his HK, "Why my Darlin' we're about to rock *this* roll. Dex—close in. Pull up along his port quarter."

Dexter glanced sideways at him. "Are you serious?"

All traces of humor left Mark's voice. "Deadly."

When Dexter hesitated, Mark sighed. "Alright, then drive up to the bumper. I'll take them out there."

"Can you take out their right rear?"

Mark was grinning again. "All day long, my man, all day long."

Dexter turned to Caterina. "Take the wheel."

As Caterina leaned over and took control of the car, Dexter climbed into the backseat and Caterina slid smoothly in front of the wheel. Dexter smiled, "You do have some moves, señorita."

Caterina smiled grimly as she closed the gap between their vehicle and the Lexus. When they were directly behind the car, Mark reached out of the window, aimed carefully and pulled the trigger. The bullet hit the tire and it exploded. The car swerved and careened against the curb to a stop.

"Drive through! Keep going!" Dexter urged from the back seat. They went through the light and Dexter saw the driver look out the window, his gun drawn, as the back door swung open.

A car filled with teenagers screeched to a stop, almost sideswiping the Legend. The driver of the Legend jumped out of the car, his gun at his side. One of the teenagers rolled down the window and shouted, "Hey Dudes, get off the damn road 'til you learn how to drive!" He gave the driver the finger as they pulled off.

The two men surveyed the area and satisfied that this was no ambush, the driver motioned for the second man to check the car. They put their guns back in their jackets.

Dexter had slipped out of the car, and while the men were engaged with the teenagers, had gone around to the back of the car and then walked towards them. The driver looked at him suspiciously.

Dexter walked over to him, seemingly oblivious and asked, "Have you seen a taxi pass by here in the last few minutes?"

The driver looked Dexter up and down and answered, "No."

Dexter continued chatting. "Yeah, I haven't either. I hate trying to get a cab in this part of town." He looked over at the second man, who was inspecting the flat tire and with a nod to the driver, walked over to him. "Need some help, buddy? Whoa, you really blew that tire out."

The second man looked over at the driver, who gave him a brief nod before climbing back into the car. The man turned back to Dexter. "Thanks. I could use a hand."

Dexter leaned in closer. "My wife's tire went out on her last month. Luckily a cop stopped and changed it for her. Knowing that woman, she'd have left the car to be stripped—course, if it had happened here, she would-n't have been able to get a taxi home."

The man continued working, "Yeah, right. Wanna help me with this?"

"Sure, sure." Dexter reached forward, placing his fingers firmly on the pressure points of the man's neck. He placed a chemical soaked cloth over his mouth and nose. The man collapsed quietly, and Dexter laid him out on the street.

The driver rolled down his window. "Hey Brad, hurry it up." When there was no response, he said again, "Brad? Brad?" Looking into his side reflector mirror, he saw the feet of his companion, splayed out on the street. Just as he pulled out his MP5 automatic weapon, there was a loud thud on roof of the car. It was Dexter. He reached down and pointed his gun at the driver. "Drop it."

The driver rolled and fired two rounds, one nicking the roof of the car. Dexter ducked.

"Head or heart, your call" Mark yelled a few feet away, his gun point-ed at the driver's head.

The driver dropped the gun as Mark moved in. Placing his knee in the small of the man's back, Mark growled, "You son of a..."

Dexter had opened the passenger door and helped Beverly out of the car. She fell into Dexter's arms, but then was pulled into a strong embrace by Mark. "Are you okay, baby?"

Dexter turned away. He walked back to the prone body of the assailants and fished into their pockets for the keys to Beverly's handcuffs. He tossed them to Mark and then leaned against the car, his back to them, surveying the streets.

Mark unlocked Beverly's hands and she flung her arms around his neck, covering his face with kisses.

Mark laughed as he pulled away and holding her face between his palms crooned. "Oh, baby. How could they ever think they could keep us apart?"

Beverly's eyes filled with tears. She smiled and hugged Mark tighter. "Oh, Mark, I knew—"

Beverly's eyes lit on Caterina, who had been standing near the rented car, but had moved closer. Beverly recognized the stricken look on Caterina's face. It was the look of a woman who had seen her man in the arms of another. Beverly stepped away from Mark, looking at him and then at Caterina again.

Mark followed her eyes and saw Caterina moving towards them, her angry eyes filled with betrayed tears. He turned to Beverly and then back to Caterina, at a loss for words. Dexter came up behind Beverly and put his hand on her shoulder. Beverly turned away from Mark. "Let's get this finished."

Dexter glared at Mark as he guided Beverly past Caterina to the rented car. He helped her in and then went back. In silence, Mark and Dexter lifted the unconscious men from the ground and put them in the back seat of their car. A crowd had started to gather. Dexter pulled out his badge and said, "Police matter, folks. Please stand clear—and thanks for your support."

Mark started towards Caterina, but she turned on her heel and with back rigid, walked proudly back to the rented car. Mark's shoulders slumped as he and Dexter followed behind.

Beverly was devastated. How could this be happening to her? She had given Mark the all love and compassion any woman could give a man. Why did he do this to her?

"*Brown eyes, I know you will always be able to get whatever you want, but that doesn't mean what you get is what you truly deserve.*" These words spoken by Beverly's Grandpa Art echoed in her mind as they entered the SUV. Grandpa Art died when she was 16, but the advice he gave her always seemed to surface when she most needed it. His words finally made sense, albeit 20 years later. She always *wanted* Mark and had him. But she did not get what she deserved. She deserved more. She *wanted* this opportunity with Tierrasanta, but it turned out to be much less than she deserved. But Beverly was not one for self pity. Life was full of choices, and she had made hers. Now it was time to move on. There would always be time to cry.

Chapter 44

They drove in tense silence for a few minutes. Finally, Beverly took a deep breath. "We have to go back and expose them."

Grateful for the opening, Mark said, "Bev, haven't you been through enough?"

Beverly's eyes narrowed in irritation. "Enough? Young kidnapped me and threatened my life. Chase is about to become this state's next governor, with Young and Chang and their drug organization, pulling the strings at his back. Have I had enough? No! Not until we do something about this."

Caterina's voice was quiet. "We are probably the only people outside of their organization that know what's going on. They won't stop hunting us until we are dead—or we stop them." She turned and looked at Beverly.

Beverly smiled slightly. "There are a few things we are going to have to discuss. But can we table our personal issues until we deal with Young? I think I know how we can stop them." Caterina nodded a silent assent to Beverly's truce.

Dexter looked at Beverly in the rear view mirror. "Let's hear it."

• • •

They pulled up in front of the RenCen. The convention was in full swing, and the place was congested with attendees milling about. A group of protesters stood outside the entrance, chanting about how unfair Chase was to the City of Detroit. A man, dressed in full African garb, was standing in the midst of them on a makeshift platform. He quieted them down and began to speak.

"This country reeks of corrupt lies and ingrained racism. Simmons has spoken out against the politics of the privileged. He speaks out about America is being raped right before our eyes and admonishes us because we act as if we are on an erotic tryst with a passionate lover. I say to you supporters of Chase' oppression, fear not the people of color, but it is your voracity that will be your undoing!" The crowd cheered wildly.

Caterina watched the crowd worriedly. "We'll never get in there. Look at the security."

Mark scanned the grounds and then said, "Dex—drop me off. I'll meet you around the back at the loading dock."

Mark got out of the car and headed over to a man wearing an Easter bunny outfit. He was waving at the conventioneers and handing out Chase buttons. Mark walked up to the bunny and after a few words, slipped the bunny a roll of cash and turned swiftly, walking around the corner. The bunny handed out a few more buttons and then followed Mark.

A few minutes later, the Bunny reappeared, strolling nonchalantly through the crowds, passing out a few buttons as he went.

"Hey—you, Rabbit! Get over here."

Mark looked around and saw a small, tidy man in a dark suit waving to him impatiently. He strolled over to him.

"We're not paying you to take breaks, bunny. Here, go into the hall and start passing as many of these out as you can. Get going." The man dropped a stack of pamphlets into the bunny's basket and followed him into the building.

Mark stuffed a couple of pamphlets into people's unwilling hands, until the little man was out of sight. He spotted the service entrance off to the right of the room and started heading in that direction. He stopped and turned near the door, handing out a few pamphlets while he scanned the surrounding area. Convinced that no one was watching him, Mark slipped through the doors and went to let the others in.

. . .

The convention floor was packed with delegates as they made their way through the crowds. On the stage was Governor Roberts, Chase and Toni and other campaign advisors and dignitaries. Beverly clutched Dexter's arm and nodded her head to the right of the stage. Mr. Young lazed arrogantly against the wall, watching the proceedings. Beverly ducked behind Dexter, her heart pounding with fear and anger. She didn't want Young to see her—not yet.

Dexter whispered to Beverly, "Look. Over there."

As they made their way over to the press area, Mark, who had circled the room, came in again through the entrance, throwing jelly beans and banners out to the amused crowd. He looked towards the stage, and stopped short. Taking off his headdress, he stared in rage at Toni, up on the stage.

Toni saw him too—and her face revealed it's shock for a moment before she recovered. Coolly, she tried to get Young's attention and then, revealing her growing panic, left the stage and went over to him. Keeping a cautious eye on Mark, she whispered in Young's ear.

Mark was about to shove his way through the crowd, when a lady stuck her hand into his basket, trying to retrieve candy and a button. Surprised, he jerked the basket away.

Startled, the woman pulled back her hand and gave Mark a dirty look. "You're a NASTY bunny!" she huffed. Then, with a sniff, she turned heel and moved back into the crowd.

Young saw Mark and then saw Beverly moving towards the reporters. Reaching into his jacket pocket and holding the small revolver he had hidden there, he moved to intercept Beverly. At the same time, Toni rushed back towards the stage as Chase moved to the podium. She tried to warn him with a tug on his arm, but he missed the signal, beginning his speech.

As attention turned to Chase, Young moved in on Beverly, who was talking to a reporter. Dexter saw Young too and Young hesitated for a moment when they made eye contact. Just then, Karen walked up to Dexter, blocking his view of Young and grabbing him by his hand as it moved up to remove the gun from his holster.

"First you turn me on and then turn me down and then you go and leave me in the middle of the night."

Dexter tried to look around her, "Uh…not now, Karen."

"'Not now?'" Karen followed Dexter's eyes and saw Beverly, her eyes lighting with understanding. With an angry smile, she continued loudly, "Oh, I understand. Of course. How are you, Mrs. Racine? Your husband was just telling me last night how *single* he was."

Beverly glanced up with a puzzled look on her face, then turned back to the reporter. Anger was replaced by confusion, as Karen took a step backward. Just then, Dexter moved swiftly, grabbing Young's left arm so he couldn't withdraw his pistol. Mark moved smoothly in and got Young's other arm. They struggled briefly, and then Dexter took out a small stun pen and stuck it into Young's ribs. Jolted, Young was unable to resist, as Mark walked him out of the hall.

Karen watched the exchange and turned to Dexter, who smiled slightly and shrugged. Karen lowered her eyes in vague apology, then turned and walked away.

Dexter walked over to Beverly and the reporter. The reporter had a skeptical look on his face as he asked, "Okay, let me get this straight. You think Toni Daniels delivered four million dollars to Chase' campaign fund to guarantee approval of the Mount Clemens project? And this alleged money comes from an international drug cartel?"

Beverly nodded her head in frustration. "Yes. The money is definitely laundered."

The reporter put his pen in his pocket and closed his notebook. "That's a pretty big accusation. No offense, but I'd need more proof than you word on something like this."

Beverly pulled the disk out of her pocket and showed it to the reporter. "This disk contains all the proof you need. But if you don't do something right now, Chase will be in office and out of our reach."

The reporter hesitated, staring at the disk in Beverly's hand, then at her face. "And I'd get the exclusive on the contents of that disk?"

Beverly smiled. "Absolutely. It is career making. Believe me."

The reporter raised his hand and shouted over the crowd, "Mr. Chase, Mr. Chase!"

Chase pointed to the reporter, as Toni grabbed Chase' shoulder and whispered nervously in his ear. "Two questions, Mr. Chase. First, will your administration increase the state sales tax by 2% as has been rumored?"

Chase smiled and lightly moved away from Toni. He leaned into the mike, his voice booming with confidence. "No. And that's a definite no. There is no reason for a sales tax increase in this quarter—or in any quarter if I have anything to do with it—it won't happen on my watch!"

The crowd applauded its approval. When the noise had died down a bit, the reporter spoke up again. "That is certainly good news, Mr. Chase. Now, my second question?"

Chase continued smiling confidently, urging the reporter to go ahead and ask his next question. The reporter's voice seemed to echo through the room as he said, "Is there any truth to the allegations that you accepted campaign funds from a South American drug cartel in return for your pushing through the Mount Clemens project?"

The room was eerily silent, as all faces turned in horror to the stage, awaiting Chase' reply. "That is absurd! I will not have you slander me, my campaign or that project which will bring needed jobs and revenue into our state with headline grabbing, unsubstantiated yellow journalism!"

Over the trickle of applause, the reporter called out, "Then how do you explain your financial consultant's timely visit to São Paulo and the four million dollar funds transfer into your war chest, hours after the announcement of Mount Clemens' approval? Funds that were transferred, conveniently, just *after* you filed your financial statement?"

Chase's face blanched, as the convention floor erupted in excitement. "There is nothing illegal about the funds in the campaign accounts. People! People please! In the interest of full disclosure, I will have my financial consultant, Ms. Daniels explain the transaction to you." He stepped away from the mic, turning to Toni, but she was gone.

Chase looked wildly around the stage and then the room, as the governor and the other dignitaries quickly exited the stage. Suddenly, through the doors leading out to the lobby, a woman's piercing scream was heard. As the conventioneers ran for the exits, Dexter grabbed Beverly's arm and pulled her away against the crowd. She handed the reporter the disk and allowed Dexter to spirit her away from the hall.

They ran through the fire exit and back through another door into the lobby. The police were pushing people away from the fountain, putting up a barricade. Through the crowd, Beverly saw Caterina, her face filled with horror. Following her glance, Beverly looked to the fountain. Her hand flew to her mouth in an effort to stifle the scream that was caught in her throat.

The bunny was lying in the fountain with his throat cut. The water spilling through the garish statue was pink with the murdered man's blood. A little girl was crying, and screaming hysterically, "Mommy, mommy! They killed the Easter bunny!"

Dexter grabbed Beverly and shoved his way across the room, pulling Caterina out of the crowd. Handing Beverly his gun and the room key, he urged them away. "Get back to the room. Don't let anyone in—use this if you have to! I'll get back to you as soon as I can. Go!"

The women staggered away from the crowd to the elevators. Dexter turned back to the fountain, as a police officer removed the head of the bunny costume.

Chapter 45

Caterina sat on the couch, fumbling with a letter opener. Beverly was perched on the windowsill, staring out at the commotion below. The street was blocked off by police cars, and orange barricades kept the milling crowds of onlookers, the conventioneers who had been herded out of the lobby and hall, and the reporters from all media. Television vans were parked across from the building, cameramen perched on top. Reporters milled about frantically shoving through the crowds with mics and cameras, searching for side stories, bits of gossip that might give their report a different angle, distraught women with tear-smudged mascara running down their faces—faces that might draw in their evening news audiences.

Beverly gasped and pressed closer to the window. Caterina looked up and rushed over in time to see two ambulance workers carry a black body bag on a stretcher out of the Center and load it into the ambulance. She swallowed hard, as the doors shut and the ambulance drove away, no lights or sirens. Their passenger was in no hurry.

Beverly moved away from the window and went to the bar. She poured herself hot tea, and then looked over at Caterina, who was standing frozen by the window, the letter opener she was holding, gripped tightly in her hands and pressed against her chest. "Can I get you anything?" Beverly asked gently.

"Mark came back here for you, and now he's dead." Caterina turned to Beverly, "Why couldn't you let him live in peace?"

Beverly was stunned. "'Let him live in peace?' Mark and I were to be married in three weeks. But somehow, you managed to turn his head. If *you* had let him be, he would never have been flying helicopters down in Brazil. He would not have taken that woman into those mountains."

Beverly advanced slowly towards Caterina. "If you had respected Mark's commitment to me, they would not have gone after him. Or me. Yes. He came back for me, because he loved me."

Caterina's eyes flashed with hurt and anger. "Mark never mentioned you! If you had been able to make him happy, he never would have come looking for me. You American women want it all. Not only do you drain a man of his love, but you demand his soul as well! You could never have made him happy, because you would never let a man like Mark be who he was born to be. And now he's dead."

Caterina turned, exhausted, away from Beverly and went to the couch. As she sank into the cushions, she continued softly, "When we first met, he told me he was in love, but he was not happy. Mark was a man with a tortured spirit. America was no true home to him, because it was not his heart's home. But he found his home in Ilhéus and it was I who gave him what his heart longed for—understanding, compassion, love...and a family." Tears spilled over Caterina's long lashes and splashed down her shirt.

Beverly took a step towards Caterina and stopped. "A family?" she whispered.

Caterina sighed heavily and wiped her tears. She looked up, her chin held proudly high. "Yes. I am carrying Mark's child. And now he will never know."

Beverly's anger melted into compassion. She knelt beside Caterina. "Oh...I had no idea. Oh Caterina...you had to have known this would be dangerous. Why did you come here in your condition?" Caterina sniffed back her tears. "Because a woman goes where her man needs her."

Beverly held her hand out to Caterina. Caterina took Beverly's hand and squeezed it tightly. Then she placed Beverly's hand on her stomach. They looked at each other and then Caterina burst into tears. Beverly took her in her arms and stroking her hair, whispered "Shhh, shhh. Everything will work out, somehow."

They separated. Caterina searched Beverly's face, her eyes hopeful that she might find the answer to how everything might work out, now that the man she loved was dead.

Beverly swallowed hard. "Mark and I were going to be married, but I knew, somehow, that it wasn't right. In my heart, I think I knew that we weren't supposed to be together. I pushed those thoughts aside. Threw them away. I had longed for Mark for so long and when we were together…but that wouldn't have been enough in the end. Caterina? I know that Mark loved you. He wanted me, yes, but he didn't look at me the way he looked at you."

Beverly laughed bitterly. "I watched his eyes watch you. Wherever you were, whatever he was doing, he was watching you. You were his treasure. And now," Beverly's voice broke, "and now you have his treasure. His child." Beverly wiped her tears and took a deep breath. "And so, you see? It has to work out. Somehow, it will all work out, Caterina. I promise you."

Just then, there was a knock at the door, breaking the tearful moment between the women. Beverly grabbed her purse and pulled out the gun.

Caterina gripped her arm. "Don't answer it," she whispered fearfully.

"It's me, Dexter," the voice called through the door.

Beverly went to door, wiping her tears. She took a last look back at Caterina, who was now standing, patting her hair in place and smoothing her clothes. Beverly opened the door.

Dexter slipped into the room and locked the door behind him. He turned and looked at the drawn and worried faces of the two women. "It wasn't Mark."

The two women just stared at him for a moment, and then Caterina let out a long keen of anguish, slipping to the floor. Beverly rushed over to her and put her arms around her, looking up at Dexter, horror and relief playing across her face. "Are you certain?"

"It was Young. I saw his face."

Caterina looked up at Dexter. "Then where is Mark?"

Dexter walked tiredly to the sofa and sat down, rubbing the fatigue from his eyes. "I don't know. Hell, he could be anywhere. My guess is he's on his way back…home."

Caterina got to her feet and moved past Beverly to the couch. She stood over Dexter and said, "Home? What are you talking about? Ilhéus?"

"That's very possible." As if to himself, Dexter continued, "I don't believe Mark killed Young, but the police certainly do. Mark had to have known they'd come after him first so, he probably got out of the city. I know that's what I would have done."

Caterina sat beside Dexter, grabbing his sleeve desperately. "But he wouldn't leave without me."

Dexter looked at Caterina and sighed. He had no answer for that. Instead he said, "Well, there's nothing else we can do here. Maybe it's time for us to get out of this town too."

Dexter glanced up at Beverly, who hadn't moved from her spot in the middle of the floor. Her face was determined as she shook her head. "We can't leave until we finish what we've started. Young is dead, but Chang isn't—and Toni has disappeared. If we don't finish this, none of us will ever be safe and Mark will be hunted forever." She looked over at Caterina. "We can't let that happen. We have to clear his name so he can—we can all move on with our lives." She turned away and went to the window.

Dexter was confused, but Caterina understood and smiled. Dexter stood and went over to Beverly, putting his arms around her gently. "You've been through a lot Beverly and you've handled everything admirably. But Mark has made his choice. He's gone. And we have to do what is best for us, now."

He turned Beverly around to face him. "I want you to know that I have never stopped caring about you. I care about you, more than you'll ever know. We have probably lost Mark, but he'll be alright. I…I don't want to lose you too, Bev."

Beverly lowered her eyes and was silent. Dexter sensed her uneasiness and let her go, taking a step backward. "You still love him, don't you?"

Beverly shook her head. "No. I mean…I don't know, Dex. Too much has happened too fast. I don't know how I feel. I'm not sure about anything right now." She looked again at Caterina. "Anything." She continued more strongly, "Except we have to finish this, Dex. I can't move on, none of us can move on, until we know it's over."

Caterina's voice was small as she said from the sofa, "They worked for a man named Tanaka. I met him only once, about six months after they helped me get out of Cuba. Such a small, quiet man, but he wielded great power. They introduced him to me that one time, so that I could pay proper respects to the man who had facilitated my escape."

Dexter looked up sharply. "Tanaka? Are you certain?"

"Yes, of course. I was summoned to the cottage, made to dress up especially pretty for him." Her voice was bitter. "They told me that I was to give myself to him "in appreciation" for his saving my life. But he didn't want me. He told them there were…better ways for me to prove my gratefulness." She looked away.

Dexter moved swiftly to the phone. "If it *was* Tanaka, then perhaps there is a way to end this." He picked up the phone and dialed Bremmer's number. "I think it is time to call in the calvary."

Chapter 46

Bremmer picked up the phone on the third ring. "Tom, it's Dexter."

Bremmer's voice rattled through the receiver. "Son of a bitch! Wait—hold a sec." Dexter heard the phone clatter against the desk and a moment later, a door slam. The receiver was picked up again and Bremmer started, "Man, where have you been? I left you a message hours ago. What the hell is going on up there? Sounds like all hell has broken loose. It's on all the stations."

Bremmer laughed, "Wanna hear the good stuff? That license you sent me? Patricia Hughes a/k/a Toni Daniels? A match. Toni Daniels: thirty-four years old. Stanford graduate with honors, CPA 1990. Campaign finance manager for the former Lt. Governor, Richard Chase. The news reports she is wanted for questioning—if they can find her."

Dexter interrupted him. "I know all of that. What I just found out— is Tanaka is neck deep in this whole thing. I think it's time to move in on this baby."

Bremmer's voice got serious. "Hold your horses man, did you say Tanaka? What's your source? We can't make a move like that without iron clad."

Dexter looked over at the two women listening in on the call. "I have the proof. But there's something else. My buddy, Mark Davis, is missing.

I have reason to believe that the only way to save him, is to bring Tanaka down. I need your help."

"Hold it. Just hold it one second. Is this a personal vendetta? Because you know I have your back man, but I'm can't put my ass on the firing line for something personal. Do you know what would happen if we got in a mix with Tanaka on a bogus hunt?"

Dexter tried to control the anger in his voice. "I know my job, Tom. And I wouldn't ask you to do this, if I didn't have sufficient cause. I'm calling you because time is short. I don't have the time to go through channels. We can bring Tanaka down, but I have to save Mark too, if I can. I understand if you can't help me. I'll go it alone if I have to. I'll take Tanaka down myself and the Secret Service be damned!"

"Hey! Hey! Alright. Jeesh. This is a big risk man, you'd better know what you're doing. I'll get a team together and get up there immediately. Don't make any moves until I get there, Rambo. Capice?"

Dexter sighed with relief. "Thanks man. I'm waiting."

• • •

Dexter, Bremmer and five veteran agents from their department, sat around the hotel room in the dark. Bremmer was standing behind a projector, the light streaming out to the wall opposite. They studied the image there—Toni Daniel's photograph and file filled the wall

"Previous employer, Kadena Industries, 1990 until 1997, when she resigned her position and transferred there to Detroit. She was immediately hired on at the State Attorney's Office where she worked until approximately eight months ago, when she resigned to take over finances for the election bid."

Agent Epstein leaned forward. "Kadena? Weren't we investigating that company at one time?"

Bremmer answered. "Right-o. It is the parent company for Deltonics and LazerData. Controlling interest held by Itari Wo, Tanaka's father-in-law."

Agent Lewis cut in, "But what does any of this have to do with Brazil or Tierrasante or this election?" He looked over at Dexter, his brow furrowed in puzzlement.

Dexter got up and stood against the wall, next to Toni's enlarged face. "That's where it gets good, my man. There is no connection. Nothing that we could prosecute with. But—Toni Daniels made several trips to Brazil on behalf of Kadena in the last two years she was with the company. Her face has shown up with various characters we have been investigating down there in connection with Tanaka and his possible associations with a drug cartel down there."

Bremmer hit the button and the picture on the wall changed. Now it was the phony license Dexter had given him. "Now, Dexter hands me a phony passport with her picture on it. Patricia Hughes has traveled to Brazil over a dozen times in the past five years. Why is she using a dummy name if her business is legitimate? Worth a little more digging.

"There was, a couple of months ago, a stirring of suspicion around illegal contributions to the Chase' campaign fund and the possibility of special interests bribing their way into a land development deal. That was just about the time Tanaka showed up on the Hill again. And just as quickly as the gossip started, it stopped—cold. The investigation died."

Bremmer grinned in anticipation. "And guess who's been tracked to Detroit on the eve of that convention?"

Dexter breathed heavily. "Tanaka."

"Tanaka."

Dexter took over. "Now I quite by accident fell into this when a friend of mine in Philadelphia called me in and I had to travel to Brazil. Mark Davis was presumed dead in a helicopter crash, but he turned up alive— and gave me the license. Things really sped up after that. My friend in Philadelphia, a real estate agent, turned up missing in Philadelphia, her work colleague executed. Both of them were associates of Tierrasante, the same company underwriting the Mount Clemens deal.

"I followed Toni Daniels here and observed her in a restaurant two nights ago. She and an unidentified male were discussing Ilhéus and something that was planned to go down here during the convention."

Bremmer clicked to the next picture. It was a police scene shot of the dead man in the bunny suit, laying in the fountain. Dexter explained, "This was taken just outside the convention hall earlier this afternoon. The corpse has been identified as Joseph Young. He is the head of the Tierrasante organization and spearheaded their land development project "Colonnade." He is also the man who kidnapped Ms. Madsen and held her hostage here in Detroit."

"I have received information that Tanaka is still here in Detroit and that he is meeting with some of his colleagues this evening here at this very hotel. One of the businessmen scheduled to meet with him is Stanley Polinski, a up and coming contractor here in the Midwest. Unfortunately, Mr. Polinski cannot make that meeting, as he is being detained for questioning regarding certain illegal activities in connection with the unions in Minnesota."

Bremmer shut off the projector. "Tanaka is a tough nut to crack. We can't tie him definitively to the Brazilian activities, however, we might be able to hold him on election tampering long enough to bring in some of the lesser players, whom I am certain will trade him in for a good deal."

Bremmer turned to Epstein. "You, will be Mr. Polinski for the evening. We don't expect you to put on an elaborate charade, but we need to get on tape, proof of Tanaka's political interference. We believe that this is what tonight's business is about. With the very possible fall of Mount Clemens, Tanaka is going to have to make a few fast moves to protect both his investments and his ass. You'll go in wired. We'll position ourselves around the restaurant and when you've gotten enough information, we'll move in. I want this to be clean and quick. I don't want to have to bring in the locals unless absolutely necessary. Dexter?"

Dexter flipped on the overhead light and handed each man a folder. "Inside you'll find photographs of tonight's players, a floor plan of the restaurant and surrounding area and more detailed information about everything we've discussed here. The meeting is at seven thirty, so we have two hours to memorize everything. We'll meet back here at six thirty sharp for final instructions before we move into position. Any questions?"

The men all shook their heads. "Fine. Then let's do it."

Chapter 47

Tanaka sipped his martini, as Chang walked towards the table. Three men followed behind him and stopped at a respectful distance as Chang bowed and addressed Tanaka.

"It is an honor to meet you, sir. Thank you for allowing me to represent Mr. Young at this meeting." Tanaka nodded his head and Chang stood up again, motioning for the men to join them.

"Gentlemen, please be seated." Tanaka waved his hand impatiently. "Time is short, so we will move to the business at hand. Chang immediately pulled a folder out of his briefcase and handed it to Tanaka. As he scanned the papers, one of the men spoke up.

"Mr. Tanaka, I've been getting calls from friends and associates wanting homes in the villages. These are people who are willing to put up quite a bit. I know you gents have your plans and all, but can't you open up at least one of those villages?"

The other two men looked at the man and then Mr. Tanaka. Chang broke in. "I'm sorry, but that is impossible. The villages are designed for those identified. As you know, the Colonnade project has been very carefully worked out to the tiniest detail. It is imperative that we continue as planned and maintain the original Colony concept. If we start making allowance now, even for one as esteemed as you, sir, the plan would collapse into chaos almost immediately."

Tanaka nodded his head. "Yes, this is true. Mr. Grandinetti, the villages will not be tampered with. We will, however, assist you in financing a project of your own, if it is prosperous, of course."

Grandinetti's face turned red with anger, but his voice was quiet as he answered, "I'm sure you would, sir. But hell, some of the people you are letting move into those villages don't strike me as being particularly desirable or even necessary."

The table was silent. Tanaka simply stared at Grandinetti without responding. When he couldn't stand the rising tension, Grandinetti said, "Fine. Then why don't you let my people buy out one of the sites. I've got people in place who would—"

Chang interjected, "The answer is no, Mr. Grandinetti. We will not sell and we will not make allowances. The villages are targeted for identified Level I and II only."

Grandinetti pushed his chair away from the table and stood. "Who the hell do you think you're dealing with here, boy?"

Tanaka raised his hands, "Please, Mr. Grandinetti, have a seat. We will table that discussion for now, but I can assure you, we will resolve it at a later time. And we will do so as gentlemen and businessmen."

Grandinetti grudgingly took his seat, glaring at Chang as he did. Tanaka resumed speaking. "Gentlemen, I have asked you to join me because I have an important matter to discuss. As you are all aware, the colloquium has enjoyed great success in the past year.

Given our accomplishments, I rarely solicit support for domestic affairs. This issue, however, threatens the economic well being of America.

"Several groups in your country have been lobbying heavily in Washington to limit foreign ownership here. There is no need, I am certain, to explain to you accomplished gentlemen, how absurd and short sighted such an idea is. Foreign investment means a vibrant, growing economy—both for your country and yourselves individually. Your immediate financial and political support in this critical matter is required and of course, greatly appreciated."

One of the men coughed loudly and reached for his water. "Excuse me, gentlemen," he sputtered through his coughs, "I will return shortly."

They watched as he made his way to the back of the restaurant and entered the men's room and then turned back to their discussion.

As the door closed behind him, Dexter stepped out and slapped him on the back. "Good work, Epstein." Dexter spoke into his headset. "Let's move in."

With guns drawn, Dexter and Epstein exited the men's room. At the entrance of the restaurant, two men stood guard. Two men, sitting at a table nearby having coffee, pushed away from their table and reached into their inside jacket pockets as they rose and moved towards Tanaka's table.

Epstein and Dexter stood over Tanaka's party. Dexter looked at Tanaka and said, "Please, continue what you were saying?"

Tanaka looked up at Dexter, his face a mask of unconcern. "Well, what have we here? Rent-a-cops?"

Dexter grinned, "Rent this, Tanaka. U.S. Secret Service. You're under arrest for conspiring to undermine U.S. financial institutions and tampering with United States elections."

Tanaka picked up his drink and finished it. After placing it neatly on its coaster, he said in a bored voice, "You seem rather arrogant. I'm surprised Secretary Davis actually sent a couple of revenuers after me."

Just then, one of the men at the table stood abruptly, hands in the air. "I want immunity from prosecution. I have a family. I'll tell you everything I know."

All activity stopped in the restaurant. Dexter looked at the man, and in that split second, the third man pulled out a gun and shot himself in the head.

The room broke out in chaos. Tables and chairs were overturned as frightened diners fought their way out of the room. Dexter motioned for his men to move in, and Chang pulled a gun from his lap and, with his hand concealed by the tablecloth, shot Epstein in the leg. The second gunshot caused a new outbreak of screaming and panic. Epstein fell to the floor in agony, and Dexter reached out to help. As he bent forward, Chang karate jabbed him in the throat and he too, fell gasping to floor.

Quickly, he urged Tanaka away from the table. They quickly melted into the mob crowding at the entrance. Dexter's men dove into the crowd searching for them, yelling into their headsets to send in backup. They didn't see Chang slip to the side of the crowd and, urging Tanaka in front of him, slip through the kitchen doors and disappear. But Dexter did.

Gasping for air, he stumbled after them. They were not going to get away.

• • •

Dexter raced through the kitchen, but there was no sign of Chang or Tanaka. The kitchen was abandoned, the workers having been evacuated earlier before gun shots were fired. Dexter raced through the room to the exit, but there were several large bags of garbage blocking the door. He turned and scanned the room and then saw another door.

Bursting through it, he found himself on the fire stairs. Above him he heard the clatter of feet running up the concrete steps. He followed them, his chest bursting with pain as he recovered from Chang's attack. "Halt! You are under arrest. Don't make this more difficult than it has to be."

Dexter heard laughter above him. A moment later, Chang's face appeared far above him. "You watch too many police shows, Mr. Racine."

As Chang continued climbing the stairs, he yelled out, "You can't possibly win, Mr. Racine. I can go anywhere in the world. Regardless of what power you think your government has, I have more! I'll make life miserable for you Dexter. You'll *wish* you were a slave in Ole Mississippi."

Chang pulled back and Dexter heard his footsteps as he continued to climb. A moment later, he leaned over the railing again. "My biggest mistake was not blowing your precious Beverly's brains out in Philadelphia. Yeah, I should have blown her fucking brains out—Bang! the gun crackled. Mr. Racine? You can be sure that *that* is the first thing I'll take care of.

Chang waved his gun over the railing and Dexter pulled back, pressing against the wall. Chang laughed and continued his ascent, yelling as he went, "I'll wait until you least expect it and then blow Beverly away and laugh as she dies in your arms. Poetic, don't you think?"

Dexter moved stealthily up the stairs, following the footfall of Chang and more distantly, the coughing, plodding steps of Tanaka, perhaps a floor above Chang. Suddenly, a garbage can was thrown over the railing, clattering loudly as it banged against metal as it made it's way down the shaft. Not knowing what the sound was, Dexter again pressed against the wall and waited. A moment later, he continued his climb.

Dexter burst through the door onto the partially renovated 72nd floor. It was dark, the only light, a dim gray filtering through the heavy plastic construction wall protecting the floor from the outside elements. He could faintly hear the approach of the FBI helicopters that were closing in, as federal forces surrounded the building hundreds of feet below.

Chang had to be on this floor, hiding. There was nowhere else for him to have gone. Checking his ammo, Dexter strained to hear movement, breathing, something. There was only the wind pushing through the seams of the temporary wall. He moved cautiously, from concrete pillar to concrete pillar, his gun up and ready to fire.

"Mr. Racine, this is a waste of your time. Don't you realize you can't stop us? This is bigger than you."

Dexter strained to identify Chang's position, but the echo effects of the large, empty space, made it impossible.

A moment later, he heard a shuffle to his left and turned quickly, positioning his gun. There was a wheeze and then Tanaka whispered, "Cut a deal with him fool. Mr. Racine? Mr. Racine, ten million dollars to walk away."

Dexter moved swiftly to the next pillar in the direction of Tanaka's voice. "No deal, Tanaka. Its over."

"Think about it, Mr. Racine. I can give you anything you want. All you have to do is report us dead and walk away."

Suddenly, there was a gunshot and a heavy thud. Dexter rolled to the floor and froze. Chang stepped from behind some crates that were stacked near the temporary wall. In the dim light, Dexter could make out the prone body of Tanaka, a widening pool of darkness spreading from his body.

"Okay Mr. Racine, one down, two to go. Give yourself a break, Tanaka can't talk now. At least I hope not! What is it that you want, Mr. Racine? A medal or something? Do you really think anyone's going to thank you for what you are doing? They will take your dead body from this building and give you a line in tomorrow's paper. After that? All you will have accomplished is your death. The Colonnade cannot be stopped. America *will* become another work colony, you know, just like Mexico. You can certainly understand that, can't you? Why not save yourself?"

A board clattered against the floor, echoing loudly. Chang turned in the direction of the sound and fired his weapon three times. Dexter crawled to the next pillar. He was only three away from Chang, who was wheeling about on his heel, swinging his gun wildly.

Dexter pointed his gun at Chang, but Chang jumped behind the pillar again. "I know you're out there, Dexter. Dexter?" Chang's voice was eerily sing-songy. "Are you—THERE?!" Chang swung out from behind the pillar and fired his gun in Dexter's direction. He pulled the trigger again. Click—his gun was empty.

"Uh, Mr. Racine, I seem to have run out of ammunition. Could you me pass some? Come on Racine, have a sense of humor."

Dexter looked cautiously around his pillar. Chang had stepped out into the open space, his silhouette darkly outlined against the translucent wall. Dexter could make out the fuzzy darkness of the city just behind Chang.

"Agent Racine? I am unarmed, see?" Chang tossed the gun away from him. It clattered loudly and spun away and out of sight. "I am turning myself over to the magnificent U.S. Secret Service. You have won, Mr. Racine. Come and claim your prize!"

Dexter stepped out from behind the pillar and faced Chang, his gun leveled between Chang's eyes. Chang laughed.

"But what have you really won, my friend. Do you really think you can stop our corporation? Read the writing on the wall. Can't you see? Capitalism is stronger than Democracy. Hell, Capitalism will *devour* democracy. You can't fill a baby's bottle with freedom, my friend. The Colonnade Project will help America by colonizing it. No need to worry about sending troops to the Balkans or world trade quotas. We'll make all those difficult decisions for you.

"And the beautiful aspect of it all, Dex my man, Americans will never know! You all can continue to wave the flag, watch TV 24 hours a day, bask in your theme park fantasies without realizing you no longer control your own destiny. Doesn't that sound fair, Mr. Racine? That's all Americans really want after all."

"That's not all we want, Chang. The history of this country proves otherwise. Some may fall for your scheme, the greedy, the rich. But not all of us. In any event, it is over. I'm taking you down. One way or another."

Chang grinned. "Are you, Agent Racine?" Chang pulled a small grenade from his sleeve and pulled the pin. "If I'm going 'down' Agent Racine, I'm taking you with me."

Chang lunged for Dexter. Dexter fired off a round as he rolled to the floor. The bullet slammed into Chang's chest. Chang staggered back, laughing against the extreme pain shooting through his body. "Oh...shit" He stared at the blood rushing from his chest forming a widening stain on his hand-stitched, linen shirt.

Suddenly the searchlights of one of the helicopters illuminated the room. Dexter saw the pain on Chang's face as his grin shifted to a stare of desperation. He focused on the grenade, still firmly held in Chang's shaking left hand. Chang struggled up on his elbows and made eye contact with Dexter. "It has been and honor and a pleasure working against you Mr. Racine. Please...Please take this as a token of my gratitude." Chang tossed the grenade at Dexter.

Dexter jumped to his feet and dove away from Chang, crashing through a plastic wall moments before the grenade went off, blowing Chang's body to pieces. The explosion caused part of the partition to collapse on Dexter, burying him under a pile of debris. He could hear agents breaking through the doorway at the far end of the floor as he lost consciousness.

• • •

"To repeat the top story of the hour, a murder was committed this afternoon at the Gubernatorial convention. The excitement began when former Lt. Governor Richard Chase was blindsided by allegations that he used over four million dollars in laundered South American drug money to finance his campaign, in return for pushing through approval on the prestigious Mount Clemens Village development.

"Following the allegation, Gerald Young, a former Chicago Gold Coast banker, was found murdered in the lobby of the Convention Center. It is unclear if the matters are related, however, our investigations reveal that Young served six months in Joliet State Penitentiary in 1976 for laundering over three hundred thousand dollars through Second Chicago Savings & Loan. Second Chicago closed its doors last year due to defaulted loans.

"Sources believe Young and Toni Moore, financial consultant to the Chase' campaign, facilitated an elaborate money laundering scheme to secure Chase' Governorship of Michigan and police are trying to locate Ms. Moore for questioning. It is not clear whether Chase, who has in fact, secured the party nomination, will fill the seat. Election officials have stated that everything is on hold until the investigation is complete. It is…excuse me, this update just in!

"Toni Moore, financial consultant to Chase' campaign has just been apprehended at the Canadian border, where it is believed she was attempting to flee prosecution. Federal marshals now have Ms. Moore in custody. A press conference is scheduled for six o'clock at police headquarters and we'll be there to cover it. Stay tuned as we bring you up to the minute details in what is surely the biggest scandal in Michigan's history. This is Charles Mansfield, reporting live from the Convention Center in Detroit. Back to you John."

Chapter 48

The hospital room was filled with flowers and balloons. The sun shone brightly through the bare windows on the four people in the room. Three standing around one in the bed, an elevated leg encased in a cast, shading Dexter's eyes from the brilliant light.

"Epstein was pretty shaken up. The Justice Department thinks they have enough to close down Tanaka's organization, but it may take them a couple of years to figure out just how large it really is."

"Well at least Tierrasante is out of business." Beverly looked thoughtful as she continued, "I have to admit, The Colonnade Project would have made me rich. It seemed like such a wonderful idea. I'm glad we were able to help bring it down before I got too involved with Young and his organization, though. It cost Stan his life and it almost cost Mark and Caterina theirs."

Caterina nodded. "You were in..." she thought for a moment, "*hot water*, is that right? Hot water yourself, Beverly." She turned to Mark and took his hand.

Mark squeezed Caterina's hand and then frowned grimly. "I would like to say I am sorry that so many people died, but I'm not. Young and Chang and Toni made my life a living hell. They held me hostage as surely as they held you, Beverly. I am glad I am free. That we are all free of them forever."

Mark put his arm around Caterina, who was nodding her head in solemn agreement, and then hugged her warmly before turning back to Dexter. "So, do you think Tanaka could have gotten away with it?"

Dexter pushed the remote control. The bed slowly raised him to a sitting position. He adjusted himself gingerly and then answered. "It wasn't just Tanaka. There had to be other entities involved. But yes, I think they could have done it. The network was so transparent that no one would have ever known. Believe it or not, most of the American members of the cartel were evenly split between old money and new money. Bremmer thinks Tanaka was selling some powerful golden parachutes to South America and other paradises. And they offered a deal that seemed too good to be true."

Beverly thought about the beautiful houses, the manicured lawns and the plans she and Stan had made for wealth and power. "It did seem irresistible. And if this hadn't happened, I—and thousands of other Americans—would have been in too deep to ever get out."

Mark stood and walked over to the window, thinking hard. He turned abruptly. "It makes me wonder who the real enemy is. I'm telling you Dex, you have to get out of this country. It's turning into pure poison, man. And I mean fast."

"Where am I supposed to go, Mark? This is *my* country. The burden has always fallen on people like us. There are no golden parachutes for the middle and lower classes. Too many of our ancestors, Black, Natives, Hispanic and White have died building this country. What am I supposed to do, give it up to some spoiled brats who *think* they own this country so they can reap the benefits. I'm not giving it up that easy. This is my country. There is no other place I'd rather be."

Mark snorted in disgust. "You and your flag. Man, they'd just as soon bury you in Old Glory. We know that better than most."

Dexter's brows knotted in anger, but before he could respond, Beverly interrupted. "Enough! Will you two please just shut up?!"

Mark and Dexter both looked at Beverly. Contritely, they looked away and muttered, "sorry...yeah, me too, man."

There was an uncomfortable silence. Caterina broke the quiet by standing and turning to Beverly. "I just don't understand this. I am *always* hungry! Will you go with me down to the cafeteria to pick up a snack?"

Mark went to her. "Do you want me to go?"

Caterina held her hand out to Beverly. "No, thank you. I need to stretch my legs. Will you come with me, Beverly?"

Beverly patted Dexter's hand as she got up and walked around the bed to the door. "Sure. Come to think about it, I'm a little hungry myself. Can we get you boys anything?"

Dexter grinned at Mark and then turned back to Beverly. "Sure. I'd like a good old *American* cheeseburger and maybe...hmmm...yes. Some sweet potato pie."

Mark rolled his eyes and laughed. "Sweet potato pie? Yeah, I guess *that is* American and that *does* sound good. Cheese fries too."

When the girls were gone, Mark went over to the bed and sat down in the chair Beverly had just vacated. "This has been a strange reunion, huh?"

Dexter smiled. "Sure has. Say, do you remember back in school when we put together that black film festival? You played Harry Belafonte from *Carmen Jones* and...what was her name? Played Dorothy Dandridge..."

"Yeah! Yeah, from *Carmen Jones*. 'Day-O, Da-a-a-a-yo! Linda Boston—"

They both chimed in, "FINE!" They burst out laughing. Dexter's face got wistful. He looked over at Mark. "We were so young, huh? We were going to be new age cowboys and save the world. Stand up for the downtrodden, restore order and then kiss our women, climb back on our trusty steeds and ride off into the sunset to fight another battle. Remember?"

"Yeah, I remember, Dex. I remember." Mark perked up, "And we did it too, didn't we?

"We did it. We sure did." They were quiet for a moment.

"So, you get out of here in a day or so. Need me to stick around?"

"It would be nice to hang together for a little while." Dexter pointed to his leg caste. "But we can't go catting for a while."

Mark chuckled. "I guess not. But you know, I think those days are good and gone. I have to admit, they were fun, but I guess it's time to grow up."

Dexter looked at Mark. "I have to admit, I'm looking forward to a little peace and quiet after all that's happened. But you know, growing up doesn't mean the adventures have to end. I thought they did, for a long time, but I know better now. We just have to pick different adventures." Dexter grinned, "Like fatherhood?"

Mark smiled widely. "Yeah. Now *that's* an adventure I really hadn't thought too much about. But it'll be good. Yeah," he said almost to himself, "it'll be really good."

• • •

Epilogue

The cab drove slowly down the tree-lined street towards Dexter's house. It pulled over to the curb and stopped. The back doors opened and Beverly and Mark stepped out. As Beverly opened the front passenger side door, Mark helped Caterina out of the back seat and then he and the cabby went to back and unloaded the trunk

Beverly stepped back as Mark rolled the wheelchair over to the opened door and then reached a strong arm in and helped Dexter shift over to the chair with a small grunt. Beverly squeezed Dexter's hand briefly and then stepped behind the chair and rolled it up the walkway.

Dexter shouted over his shoulder, "You got those bags, man?"

Mark grinned and said, "As usual, I am taking care of everything. You just roll your royal behind inside and get some coffee on."

Dexter laughed. "Coffee? I think we need deserve more than that. What do you think, Bev?"

Beverly thought for a moment. "Well, I don't know about you guys, but I think champagne for the girls, eh Caterina?

"Well, just maybe a small sip." Caterina looked down at her belly and patted it. "What do you say *niño*? Can we handle a little champagne?" She waited a moment and then continued. "He says 'yes', but none of that cheap stuff."

They all laughed and Beverly continued pushing the chair up to the front door. "Oh, and Mark, pay the cabby. And give him a good tip, too."

Beverly took the key from Dexter and opened the door. "Cat? Don't you dare touch those bags in your condition. Let that man of yours get them. You come on in and get comfortable."

Caterina looked at the bags around Mark's leg. "That's true. I *am* in a delicate condition. I can track down international killers, race across a strange city dodging bullets, but I have to draw the line somewhere, yes?" She followed Beverly and Dexter into the house, giving Mark a last loving smile. "You can handle it, can't you cowboy?"

Mark sighed and turned to the cabby. "How much was that?"

"Fifty-six dollars—not including the tip, sir."

"FIFTY-SIX—" Mark looked up at the house. "Hey…aw, shoot." He turned back to the cabby as he pulled out his wallet.

"Hey man, don't sweat it, I take Visa, MasterCard and American Express."

Mark did a double take. "That's quite alright, slick. I'll pay cash."

"If you say so. But you'd better get with the program, man. Credit cards are the wave of the future and it sure makes my job a whole lot safer."

"You ever stop to wonder where the money comes from?" Mark asked.

"Nope, and don't care."

The cabby climbed into the car and shifted into gear. He leaned out the window and said, "Hey, If you need one, I got a friend who can get you a pre-approved card overnight. No questions asked."

Mark gave the cabby a wry smile. "That's the part that scares me. Thanks but I'll pass." He watched as the cabby pulled off and then picked up the bags and walked into Dexter's home.

Printed in the United States
70198LV00003B/298